PHANTOM NARVIS

CASSANDRA DOON

"When shall we three meet again
In thunder, lightning, or in rain?"
*- **William Shakespeare***

CHAPTER ONE

SEINNA

I was nestled in the middle of the bed, cocooned in a tangle of sheets faintly scented with sea salt and sweat— a comforting reminder of the ocean breeze drifting through the open window. The sheet clung to my skin, warm and familiar, embracing me softly. My body lingered in that delicious state between sleep and wakefulness, where everything felt slow, dreamlike. My muscles were heavy, relaxed with the remnants of sleep, and I wasn't ready to break free from the cocoon just yet. The outside world could wait. Here, within the safety of this bed, I was sheltered—surrounded by them.

A low chuckle broke the stillness beside me. I didn't need to open my eyes to know who it was. The weight of an arm draped lazily over my waist, fingers tracing slow, absent-minded circles on my skin. Landon. His presence was as familiar as my own breath, his teasing a constant in the early morning haze. His touch was light, playful, but grounding— anchoring me to the moment.

"Morning, sunshine," he murmured, his voice gravelly and

thick with the lingering traces of sleep. There was a lazy warmth to it that made my heart flutter. "Dream about me?"

A smile tugged at my lips, though I kept my eyes closed. "Why dream about you when you're always hogging the bed?"

His soft laugh rumbled against my back, a sound both comforting and mischievous. Landon had a way of turning even the quietest moments into something lighter, something that made the world feel a little less heavy. He shifted closer, his breath warm on the back of my neck, sending a soft shiver down my spine. "Maybe I hog the bed because you keep migrating to my side," he whispered, his voice low, playful, and full of mischief.

I rolled over to face him, opening my eyes just enough to catch the amused glint in his. His blue eyes, still heavy with sleep, sparkled with that familiar teasing light that was uniquely his. Even in these early, vulnerable moments, Landon had an effortless charm that radiated from him. His blonde hair was a tousled mess, wild and untamed from the night, but somehow, it only added to the trouble he carried with him—the kind of trouble I'd long ago learned to love.

He looked like the chaos I could never stay away from, a storm wrapped in a smile. And as he grinned down at me, I remembered exactly why I loved mornings like this.

Because with Landon, no matter how much everything else was falling apart, there was always room for light.

Before I could reply, the mattress shifted gently behind me, and a familiar presence made itself known as a strong arm slid around my waist from the other side. The weight of it was steady, deliberate—comforting in the way only Aiden could be. I didn't need to turn to know it was him. He always moved with that quiet, purposeful grace, as if even in sleep, he was calculating—grounding us all with his unwavering calm.

His embrace was different from Landon's playful touches. Where Landon teased and coaxed laughter from me, Aiden's touch was solid, protective, an anchor in the chaos of the world. His hand rested firmly on my side, the warmth of his body seeping into mine, dissolving any lingering tension. It was as if he sensed the excitement Landon stirred up and knew exactly how to bring me back to center.

"You wish," Aiden mumbled, his breath warm against my hair, his voice low and thick with sleep. There was a rawness to his early morning voice—softer than usual, but still carrying that steady weight that always made me feel safe.

I let myself melt into him, allowing the strength of his presence to calm me. Where Landon brought energy and spontaneity, Aiden offered peace. He was my rock, the one who kept everything balanced. Even when softened by sleep, his dark brown eyes carried an intensity that felt like reassurance, a silent promise that as long as he was there, nothing could touch us.

His dark hair, still somehow perfectly in place after a night of sleep, brushed against my cheek as he leaned in, pressing a tender kiss to my temple. Such a small gesture, but it meant everything—an unspoken connection, a reminder that we were exactly where we were meant to be.

"Morning," I murmured, a smile tugging at my lips. This was our rhythm—waking up in a tangle of limbs and warmth, sharing quiet moments before the world dragged us into whatever adventure awaited. The closeness between us went beyond words, a connection that defied the usual definitions of love.

We didn't need to explain our relationship to anyone. It was ours, and that was all that mattered.

"You two lovebirds done hogging all the attention?" a familiar voice drawled from the left side of the bed, unmistakably teasing.

Jax, of course. Always ready to stir things up, even at dawn.

I turned my head just in time to see Jax sitting up, stretching his arms overhead in a slow, languid motion that made his shirt ride up, revealing the defined lines of muscle along his abdomen. He moved with that easy confidence that was purely his—always the first to rise, always ready to charge into whatever chaos the day held. His jet-black hair was a tangled mess, sticking up in wild tufts from a restless night, but on Jax, it fit—an extension of his untamed spirit.

His dark eyes, half-lidded with sleep, still held that familiar wild spark that never dimmed, even in quiet moments. The way he looked at me always felt like a dare, as if he were challenging me to keep up with whatever madness brewed behind those eyes. That was Jax—restless energy and reckless abandon, wrapped in a wicked grin.

"You two keep it up, and I'll start getting jealous," Jax teased, his voice dripping with playful mischief as he flashed me a grin—equal parts charm and trouble. That grin—the kind that promised adventure, the kind that made you forget consequences, even if just for a moment.

I rolled my eyes, though I couldn't stop the smile tugging at my lips. "Jealous? You were too busy hogging all the pillows last night to notice anything."

Jax flopped back onto the bed, sprawling out lazily at my feet. "Can't help it if I need my beauty sleep," he shot back with a shrug, though the smirk never left his face. Jax was always like that—effortless, always pushing boundaries without trying. His presence crackled with energy, like he was constantly one step away from pulling us into another daring escapade. He thrived on it—the thrill of the next reckless decision.

Maybe it was that edge of danger, that raw unpredictability, that had drawn me to him in the first place. Jax was the fire that kept us from getting too comfortable, the one who made sure life never felt stagnant. He dared us to go further, to push beyond what we thought we could handle.

The four of us had been together for over three years now, and somehow, we'd found our rhythm. Landon kept us laughing, Aiden kept us grounded, Jax kept us on our toes, and me... well, I was the glue that held it all together, even if I didn't always know how. It wasn't perfect, but it was ours, and that made it enough. More than enough.

"Any big plans today, or are we staying in bed all day?" I teased, letting the thought of a lazy, indulgent morning spread through my limbs.

Before anyone could respond, I felt the weight of Aiden's gaze settle on me, his presence behind me steady as ever. He hesitated for a moment before finally speaking, his voice thoughtful. "Actually, I've been thinking."

I groaned, half-playfully, already knowing that "thinking" spelled trouble. "That's never a good sign."

Aiden smirked, his arms tightening slightly around my waist, his breath warm against my neck. "No, really. I've been doing some research. You know the Bermuda Triangle?"

My heart skipped a beat, the shift in the room palpable. "Of course. Who doesn't?"

It was a challenge—a spark. And I knew, from the way Aiden's voice dipped into that serious tone, that whatever he had planned wasn't going to be ordinary.

It was going to be one of those adventures—the kind that Jax craved, Landon joked about, and Aiden always, always approached with calculated precision.

"There's talk of a shipwreck—old, undiscovered, and near the outskirts of the Triangle." His voice dropped, as if laying out a secret.

Jax's eyes lit up instantly, a wild grin spreading across his face, his excitement almost tangible. "You're serious? The Bermuda Triangle? Tell me you want to check it out."

Aiden, calm and composed as always, nodded. "It's not deep into the Triangle, so it's relatively safe. But close enough that it could be… interesting."

I could practically feel Jax's energy buzzing beside me, as if he was ready to bolt out the door at any second. This was what he lived for—the thrill of the unknown, the edge of danger that always accompanied our explorations. For the four of us, this wasn't just a hobby; it was our life. We were deep-sea divers, and when we weren't hired for ship retrievals and salvage operations, we spent our days off hunting for undiscovered shipwrecks. It wasn't just work; it was an obsession—an adrenaline rush that coursed through our veins and kept us coming back for more.

We'd been diving for years, retrieving everything from lost cargo to sunken vessels, with calls always coming in from clients needing something pulled from the ocean's grasp. But on days like today, when we weren't answering anyone else's calls, we answered the call of the ocean itself, always searching for something no one else had found. Shipwrecks, forgotten relics, ancient stories buried beneath the waves—they were all waiting for someone to uncover them. And that someone was us.

And if I was being honest with myself, I craved it too. That heart-pounding rush of adrenaline, the thrill of plunging into the depths and pushing boundaries, of knowing we were chasing something that had remained hidden from the world. There was nothing quite like it. The rush of discovering the unknown was intoxicating, and I knew I wasn't the only one who felt that way.

Landon sat up slowly, his usual playful grin faltering as he processed Aiden's suggestion. "I don't know, man. The Triangle's got a bit of a... reputation."

He wasn't wrong. The Bermuda Triangle had a long, infamous history—ships disappearing without a trace, planes vanishing into thin air, unexplained phenomena. It wasn't exactly the safest place to hunt for shipwrecks. But that was the appeal, wasn't it?

Aiden raised an eyebrow, his gaze steady on Landon. "Since when do you shy away from adventure?"

Landon let out a dramatic sigh, draping his arm over my shoulders and pulling me close. "I don't," he said, his tone light but his grin more subdued than usual. "I just prefer keeping all my limbs intact, you know?"

I leaned into him, feeling his warmth, but the familiar buzz of excitement was already building in my chest. This was what we lived for—the thrill of the unknown, the chance to uncover something no one else had ever seen. And it wasn't just about me. It was about all of us. Each of us brought something unique, and together, we made it work. That's what made us unstoppable.

"I think we should go for it. We've got six days off, after all," Jax chimed in, his eyes gleaming with that reckless enthusiasm so uniquely his. "We'll be legends if we find something out there. Our names on the map, a shipwreck no one else has touched."

I couldn't help but grin, glancing from Jax's wild energy to Aiden's calm determination, then to Landon's thoughtful expression. They were waiting for me to tip the balance. I was always the one they looked to when the stakes were high. And if there was one thing I knew about us, it was that we thrived on risk. This was our life, and we were damn good at it.

""I think..." I paused, feeling the weight of their eyes on me. My pulse quickened, that familiar rush of excitement spreading through me like wildfire. "We'd better start packing."

Jax whooped, leaping out of bed with more energy than anyone should have this early in the morning. "This is going to be insane!" he shouted, already darting around the room, gathering his gear like we were leaving that very second.

Landon chuckled, his grin returning as he leaned down and pressed a soft kiss to my lips. "You always know how to keep things exciting, don't you?"

I smiled against his lips, my heart racing now, the thrill of adventure already sinking in. This was what we did best—diving headfirst into the unknown and coming out with stories no one else could tell.

Aiden, ever the planner, kissed the top of my head, his voice steady in my ear. "Don't worry. I'll plan everything. We'll be fine."

As I glanced around the room, watching them move with their usual mix of chaos and purpose, a flicker of doubt crept in, gnawing at the edges of my thoughts. I pushed it aside. Maybe it was how calm Aiden had been when he mentioned the Bermuda Triangle, or maybe it was the spark in Jax's eyes, something wild, like he was chasing something even he couldn't fully grasp.

Whatever it was, it tugged at me, even as excitement bubbled to the surface. The Bermuda Triangle wasn't like the other places we'd explored. It felt different, bigger, more dangerous. I couldn't shake the feeling that this was more than just another adventure.

As we packed up, ready to set sail on what promised to be one of our most thrilling ventures yet, I couldn't help but wonder if we were biting off more than we could chew. Something about this felt different. A quiet, nagging voice at the back of my mind whispered: This might not be like the others.

This time, we might not all make it back.

CHAPTER TWO

SIENNA

The sun was just rising, casting the world in soft hues of pink and gold as it broke over the horizon, bathing the harbor in a quiet glow. Early light reflected off the water, turning the calm waves into shimmering ribbons that danced around the hull of our boat. The air was crisp, carrying the salty tang of the sea, and the rhythmic sound of waves lapping against the dock should have been soothing. Yet there was an undercurrent of tension I couldn't shake. We were heading into uncharted waters, both literally and figuratively.

We had set out early—first thing in the morning, the sky barely waking. It would take the better part of the day to reach the edge of the Bermuda Triangle. Aiden's plan was simple: we'd sail straight through open water, anchor just on the outskirts of the Triangle, and spend the night there, suspended between safety and the mystery ahead. We'd rest, gather ourselves, and make the dive at first light.

Behind me, Jax was putting on a dramatic show of readying the dive gear. Fins, masks, oxygen tanks—all clattered into a pile on deck with his usual unnecessary enthusiasm, as if we weren't about to head into one of the most notoriously dangerous parts of the ocean. Jax's energy was contagious, and despite the nervous buzz in my stomach, I found myself smiling. He thrived on moments like this, the reckless anticipation of the unknown.

"This is gonna be wild," Jax said, his eyes gleaming with that dangerous mix of excitement and confidence. He flashed me his signature grin, the kind that made it seem like he was always one step away from diving headlong into trouble. "You sure you're ready for this, Sienna?"

I shot him a playful glare. "You're asking me if I'm ready? I'm always the one dragging your reckless ass out of trouble, remember?"

Jax chuckled, tossing a coil of rope over his shoulder like it weighed nothing. "Fair enough," he said, his grin widening. "Just don't slow me down when we find that wreck."

"Don't worry," I teased, leaning against the railing. "I'll be there to save you when you inevitably do something stupid."

He gave me a mock salute before turning back to the gear, but something in his eyes caught my attention. His usual carefree excitement was still there, but beneath it, something deeper stirred. A hunger. It wasn't just the thrill of the dive that had him buzzing—he was chasing something bigger, something more than just the next adventure. The realization made my chest tighten slightly. Jax was always reckless, but this felt different.

I turned back toward the boat, where Landon lounged casually against the railing, arms crossed, head tilted back like he didn't have a care in the world. His sunglasses perched on the bridge of his nose, hiding his eyes, but I knew him well enough to see through the act. He wasn't as relaxed as he looked. He might joke and play it cool, but when things got real, Landon always felt the weight of it—probably more than any of us.

"Still think we're gonna end up in the Twilight Zone?" I nudged him gently with my elbow.

He tilted his head toward me, lifting his sunglasses just enough to meet my gaze. Those familiar blue eyes held that playful glint, but beneath it, concern lurked. He gave me a half-smile. "Oh, I'm sure we'll be fine," he said, his tone light but edged with tension. "As long as you keep Aiden from overthinking and maybe stop Jax from diving off the boat the second we hit open water."

I laughed, shaking my head. "You know that's a full-time job, right?"

Landon chuckled, though the tension lingered in his voice. He could act carefree, but deep down, he understood the risks better than anyone. He might not say it, but I knew he felt the weight of where we were going, of what could happen if things went wrong. The Bermuda Triangle wasn't just another shipwreck site. It was infamous for a reason. And despite the bravado we all wore, the unspoken tension hung in the air.

As we prepped the boat, a nervous energy buzzed at the back of my mind. Aiden stood by the helm, calm and focused, running through final checks on the navigation systems. He'd mapped the route meticulously, ensuring we'd reach the Triangle's edge by sunset—just enough time to anchor and settle in before darkness fell. As always, Aiden was the planner, the one who kept us grounded, balancing Jax's wild energy and Landon's easygoing charm with his quiet intensity.

I found myself watching him, appreciating how he carried the weight of these decisions with quiet strength. He hadn't shown any hesitation, but I knew he was aware of the risks. Aiden always was. He calculated every move, making sure we didn't push too far, even when Jax and Landon were ready to leap into the unknown. His responsibility to keep us safe was something he never took lightly.

I walked over to him, my eyes tracing the tension in his shoulders as he hovered over the map. His dark hair, meticulously pulled back into a neat knot, was beginning to come loose, stray strands framing the sharp lines of his face. His jaw was set, muscles rippling beneath his black shirt as his fingers moved methodically across the chart, double-checking everything with the steady precision that defined him.

"Everything look good?" I asked softly, leaning against the railing beside him, the evening air still and quiet around us.

Aiden didn't glance up, his brow furrowed in concentration as he studied the map. His fingers traced the coordinates with deliberate care, like they carried the weight of something much bigger than a simple course. "Everything's fine," he murmured, though there was a slight edge to his voice. "The coordinates are solid. If the weather holds, we'll hit the outskirts of the Triangle by late afternoon."

I watched him more closely, noticing the flicker of something in his expression—a subtle uncertainty he was trying hard to mask. Aiden never second-guessed himself. He was always the calm center, planning every detail with unwavering confidence. But the Bermuda Triangle had a way of unsettling even the most grounded among us.

"You're sure about this, right?" I asked, studying his profile, catching the way his jaw tightened ever so slightly. "We've done crazy things before, but this feels… different."

For a moment, Aiden was silent, his eyes locked on the

chart like it held the answer to an unspoken question. Then, slowly, he lifted his gaze, his dark eyes meeting mine. In that brief exchange, his usual intensity softened, and I saw a rare vulnerability slip through the cracks of his carefully maintained composure.

"I'm sure," he said quietly, though his voice carried a heaviness that belied his words. "But I'd be lying if I said I wasn't a little nervous. The Triangle has its reputation for a reason."

There it was. The admission I hadn't expected. Aiden, who was always the one to keep us grounded, who never let fear cloud his judgment, was admitting to being nervous. I felt a shiver run down my spine, the unease that had been simmering beneath the surface now clawing its way up, settling in my chest. If Aiden was nervous, then this really was different.

I nodded, pushing away the doubt and trying to focus on what we knew. We'd been through worse, hadn't we? I trusted Aiden more than anyone, and if he thought we could handle this, then we could. "We'll be fine," I said, my voice firmer than I felt. "We always are."

Aiden's lips curved into a small, almost imperceptible smile, the kind that always made my heart flutter, even after all the time we'd spent together. "I know," he said, his voice softening. "Just… be careful, okay?"

I raised an eyebrow, smirking as I leaned in a little closer. "I should be the one telling you that."

He exhaled softly, a small chuckle escaping his lips as he shook his head. Then, before I could say anything else, he pulled me into his arms, his grip firm yet gentle, like he was anchoring both of us in that moment. The world around us seemed to fall away, leaving just the steady rhythm of the waves and the comforting warmth of his embrace. For a few precious seconds, everything felt still, like nothing could touch us.

But even in that calm, I could feel the tension thrumming beneath his skin. Aiden wasn't one to show fear, but I knew him too well. He carried the weight of every decision, every risk, like it was his sole responsibility to keep us all safe. And now, as we stood on the precipice of something unknown, I could see the burden settling on his shoulders.

"Alright, lovebirds, break it up!" Landon's voice rang out from the front of the boat, shattering the moment. I turned to see him leaning casually against the bow, flashing that trademark lopsided grin. "We've got an ocean to conquer!"

Aiden let out a low chuckle, loosening his hold on me before returning to the map. His serious expression returned almost instantly, slipping back into his role as the responsible one, the leader. "I'll finish plotting the course," he said, his voice steady and focused once more. "You go make sure Jax hasn't decided to launch himself into the water yet."

I rolled my eyes, a smile tugging at my lips as I headed toward the bow, where Jax paced like a caged animal, practically vibrating with excitement. His energy was always electric before one of our dives, but today, something felt even more intense. He thrived on moments like this—the anticipation, the unknown. For Jax, the more dangerous, the better.

"Ready to go overboard?" I teased, crossing my arms as he halted mid-pace, his dark eyes gleaming with that familiar reckless glint.

"More than ready," Jax replied, flashing me a wild grin. The excitement in his voice was palpable, as if he were just barely holding himself back from jumping into the ocean right then and there. "This is going to be epic. I can feel it."

I didn't doubt him. There was always something electric in the air before our adventures, like the energy crackled just beneath the surface, ready to explode. But today, it felt sharper, more dangerous. The Bermuda Triangle wasn't just another shipwreck site; it was something else entirely. Its reputation alone was enough to send a chill through even the most seasoned explorers, and we were no strangers to pushing limits.

"Let's just try to keep things under control this time," I said, casting him a sidelong glance, trying to inject humor into the tension hanging between us. "No need to break any bones on day one."

Jax shrugged, his grin unwavering. "Where's the fun in control?"

Before I could respond, Aiden's voice cut through the air, calm but commanding. "Sienna, Jax, we're ready. Let's get moving."

As I turned back toward Aiden, the unease settled into my chest once more. We were about to venture into uncharted waters—both literally and figuratively—and despite our bravado, I couldn't shake the feeling that this time, danger wasn't just hypothetical. This time, we might truly be in over our heads.

With a final glance at Jax, I made my way to the front of the boat, taking my place next to Landon. He threw an arm around me, his carefree smile lifting my spirits despite the nagging worry clawing at the back of my mind.

"We're really doing this, huh?" Landon said, adjusting his sunglasses before giving me a quick kiss. "Off to the Triangle. Hope you packed your lucky charm."

I laughed. "I've got you, don't I?"

"That's right, babe," he replied, flashing that playful grin that always made me feel like everything would be okay, no matter how crazy things got. "We've got this."

The engine roared to life, and slowly, we pulled away from the dock, the open ocean stretching before us like an endless, untamed frontier. The breeze whipped through my hair as the boat sliced through the water, and despite the unease gnawing at my gut, I couldn't help but feel a familiar thrill rising inside me.

We were explorers, after all. We thrived on the unknown.

But as I gazed out at the horizon, the sun climbing higher in the sky, a chill ran down my spine. I couldn't shake the feeling that this time, the unknown might be more than we bargained for.

CHAPTER THREE

SIENNA

The sun sank lower, its golden light stretching thin across the ocean's surface, casting long, soft shadows over the rolling waves. The horizon blurred where the water met the sky, an endless expanse stretching out in every direction, making the world feel both infinite and isolating. Hours had slipped by since we left the safety of the coastline behind, and with each passing minute, the weight of isolation grew heavier. Out here, it was just us and the sea—no landmarks, no signs of civilization—only the steady pulse of the ocean and the low hum of the boat's engine beneath our feet.

We were approaching the spot where we'd drop anchor for the night, settling just outside the Bermuda Triangle's edge. Tomorrow, we'd dive—if everything went according to plan. I stood at the bow, letting the salty wind whip through my hair, the cool breeze a stark contrast to the rising heat of anticipation simmering within me. Something about today felt different, heavier, like the calm before a storm. That gnawing sense of danger clung to the air, mingling with the thrill of the unknown that had lured us out here in the first place.

Behind me, Landon lounged against the railing, his posture relaxed as always, but I could sense the nervous energy radiating from him as his fingers tapped idly against the metal. Still, he never let on. His easy grin was firmly in place, his bright blue eyes sparkling with their usual playful mischief. "Think we'll actually find something, or did Aiden just drag us out here for a romantic ocean getaway?" he teased, his voice slicing through the stillness.

I smirked, glancing over my shoulder at him. "I don't know," I replied, playing along, "maybe this is just his elaborate way of setting the mood."

Landon chuckled, his laugh rich and warm, almost too carefree for the treacherous waters surrounding us. But that was Landon—always finding a way to lighten the mood, no matter how tense the situation became. It was one of the many things I loved about him. Even when the stakes were high, and the unknown loomed ominously on the horizon, he had a way of making it all feel like just another adventure. He possessed that rare gift—a talent for diffusing fear without even trying.

In stark contrast to Landon's playful spirit, Aiden stood at the helm, his gaze locked firmly on the horizon, his body taut with focus. His dark hair, neatly tied back, still betrayed a few loose strands that had fallen forward, framing his intense features. Those brown eyes of his were a deep well of concentration as they scanned the water ahead, unyielding and unwavering. The tension in his jaw was palpable, and I noticed the way his fingers gripped the wheel with a slightly tighter hold than usual. He hadn't said much since we left the harbor; his mind was clearly occupied with thoughts only he could decipher—a plan, a calculation, always strategizing ten steps ahead to ensure everything was in its rightful place. Aiden was methodical like that. Where Landon kept us laughing, Aiden kept us on course.

Jax, on the other hand, matched the excitement building inside me. He sat cross-legged near the edge of the boat, his dark hair whipping wildly in the wind, eyes wide with eager anticipation. Jax was born for this—the thrill of the chase, the rush of pushing boundaries. Every part of him buzzed with exhilaration, his entire body practically vibrating with raw energy. The wild gleam in his eyes was unmistakable, as if he were already envisioning the glory of discovering something no one else had before. For Jax, this was more than just an adventure—it was a chance to leave his mark, to prove we could conquer whatever challenges the sea threw at us.

"This is it, guys," Jax exclaimed, his voice brimming with barely contained enthusiasm as he leapt to his feet. His gaze swept eagerly over the water, excitement radiating from him. "I can feel it. We're gonna find something out here—something big."

I opened my mouth to respond, caught in a whirlwind of exhilaration and the gnawing edge of uncertainty that clung to the air like a storm cloud, when Aiden's voice sliced through the moment, low and commanding. "We've got something."

The seriousness in his tone snapped me from my reverie, the kind of tone Aiden reserved for moments of certainty. Instantly, we all turned toward him, the playful energy dissipating like mist in the morning sun. My pulse quickened as I edged closer to Aiden, who stood steadfast, eyes still fixed on the horizon.

At first, there was nothing to see—just the same endless

stretch of ocean and sky that had surrounded us all day, a vast expanse of blue fading into twilight. But as we sailed a little further, a massive shape began to emerge in the distance. Faint at first, it shimmered like a mirage in the dimming light. My breath caught in my throat as details slowly sharpened, revealing the hulking silhouette of something unnatural—something manmade.

"What the hell?" Landon muttered, stepping forward to get a closer look. His usual humor evaporated, replaced by a sense of awe.

The sun sank lower now, its last rays casting an eerie glow over the object ahead, turning the water around it a deep, foreboding shade of red. As we drew nearer, the shape transformed into something unmistakable. It wasn't merely a rock formation or a trick of the light; it was a ship—a massive, looming structure that seemed to defy logic, floating silently on the water like a ghost from another era.

Jax was the first to react, a wild grin exploding across his face. "I told you!" he exclaimed, practically bouncing on his feet with exuberance. "I told you we were gonna find something epic!"

I glanced at Aiden, whose expression remained inscrutable, yet his eyes betrayed a flicker of unease that settled deep within him like a stone. This wasn't just a shipwreck. This was something more—something none of us were prepared for.

It was a ship. A huge one.

Not the small, sunken wreck we'd anticipated diving to. This was a massive cruise liner, eerily still, floating ghostlike in the water. The ship loomed large, its hulking form casting an ominous shadow over the ocean as the sun dipped lower, painting the sky in hues of orange and violet. The closer we drew, the clearer it became—this vessel was abandoned.

Or at least, it appeared abandoned.

"There's no way," Jax breathed, his voice filled with awe, his eyes widening in disbelief as he took in the impossible sight before us. "Where did this thing come from?"

None of us had an answer. We stood there, rooted in place, gazing at the colossal cruise liner that loomed over us, completely out of context, as if it had materialized from thin air. There were no signs of distress—no flickering lights, no sounds of life, no movement at all. It was simply there, silent and still, casting an imposing shadow over the water as the sun sank deeper into the horizon.

Aiden maneuvered our boat alongside the enormous vessel, his brow furrowed in concentration as he scrutinized the ship's pristine condition. "It doesn't make sense," he muttered, his voice low and thoughtful, the weight of his words hanging in the air. "There shouldn't be anything out here. No scheduled routes. No known ships anywhere in this area."

The ship, though clearly aged, gleamed eerily in the fading light, as if it had been untouched by time itself. The hull shone with a polished sheen, windows intact and reflecting the last rays of the sun, while the paint, only slightly worn in places, whispered of a forgotten elegance. It was like a relic from another era, preserved yet untouched, frozen in time—a haunting beauty against the backdrop of the darkening sea.

"I don't like this," Landon said from behind me, his usual humor evaporating into genuine unease. He leaned forward, squinting up at the liner, his easygoing demeanor replaced by a taut seriousness. He wasn't wrong—the sight of that massive ship sent an icy shiver down my spine, and I struggled to shake it off. The silence enveloping it, the way it loomed so perfectly still, as if waiting for something—or someone—unnerved me more than I cared to admit.

Jax, however, was undeterred, a wide grin spreading across his face like sunlight breaking through clouds. His eyes practically sparkled with excitement. "This is incredible!" he exclaimed, practically bouncing on his feet. "We have to check it out."

Landon shot him a disbelieving look, his discomfort palpable. "Check it out? Are you insane? That thing looks like it's been sitting here for decades. No way this is a good idea."

"Exactly!" Jax replied, his grin widening further, infectious in its enthusiasm. "That means whatever's inside has been untouched for ages. Can you imagine what we'll find? This could be the discovery of a lifetime!"

I turned to Aiden, my pulse racing as I awaited his verdict. His jaw was clenched tight, and his gaze remained fixed on the ship, revealing the internal battle raging within him. The logical side of Aiden—the part that valued safety and control—was urging him to turn back, to seek the familiar over the unknown. But the adventurer in him, the very essence that had propelled him to explore the mysteries of the world for years, was drawn irresistibly to the enigma before us.

After what felt like an eternity of silence, Aiden finally spoke, his voice steady but resolute. "We'll check it out," he declared, and my heart leaped at his decision. "But we stay together. No splitting up. We don't know what's on board."

Jax erupted into cheers, already seizing the rope to secure our boat to the side of the cruise liner, his excitement spilling over like the waves lapping against the hull. Landon let out a resigned sigh, rubbing a hand over his face as if trying to wipe away his apprehension. "This is how horror movies start, you know."

I shot him a playful smirk, nudging him lightly. "Don't worry," I teased. "If this turns into a horror movie, I'll make sure you're the last one standing."

Landon chuckled, the tension in his shoulders easing just a fraction. "Damn right," he replied, his trademark confidence flickering back to life, though I could still see the shadow of unease lingering in his eyes.

As we secured our boat to the cruise liner, a strange cocktail of excitement and dread surged within me. This wasn't part of the plan, but when had we ever adhered to the plan? The sight of the massive ship loomed over us, its eerie yet regal presence sending prickles across my skin. It felt too pristine— too perfectly preserved. There should have been signs of wear and decay, yet everything appeared untouched, as if it had been waiting for our arrival, beckoning us into its silent embrace.

We ascended the rope ladder to the deck, the wood beneath our feet groaning softly with each step. The air was thick with an oppressive silence, pressing in from all sides and amplifying every sound. I glanced around, absorbing the details as I cautiously crossed the deck. The ship, though old, bore no signs of abandonment. The railing gleamed, and the floors were mostly intact. There were rust stains here and there, a few cracks in the windows, but overall, the liner appeared in far better condition than it had any right to be.

"This place is huge," Jax exclaimed, spinning in a slow circle, his eyes alight with wonder. His excitement stood in stark contrast to the unease that gripped the rest of us. "It's like a ghost ship."

He wasn't wrong. The vessel felt abandoned, but not in the

usual sense. It wasn't decayed, dilapidated, or overrun by nature. It was almost... preserved. As if it had been left here intentionally, waiting for someone to uncover its secrets. But for how long? And why?

Aiden's voice sliced through the stillness, his tone sharp and commanding. "Stay close," he warned, his gaze sweeping the length of the deck. "We don't know what we're dealing with."

This wasn't just another dive; something about this place felt profoundly different. It felt alive, as if the ship itself were watching us, anticipating our next move.

We pushed through the main doors and stepped into the ship's interior. The deeper we ventured, the more a sense of wrongness settled over us, heavy and palpable. It was like entering another realm—one suspended in time. The first room we entered was the main lounge, a sprawling space adorned with velvet couches and grand, ornate chandeliers hanging from the ceiling. Everything appeared immaculate, as if the ship had been prepared for guests only moments ago. It was unsettlingly perfect. Too perfect.

The eerie stillness clung to the air as our eyes roamed the room. Glasses of half-drunk wine sat on the tables, their crimson liquid gleaming under the dim light, untouched by time. Luggage was scattered haphazardly across the floor, open suitcases spilling clothes as if the passengers had been interrupted mid-unpacking. Yet, there were no people—no crew bustling about, no passengers savoring their drinks. Just silence. Complete and utter silence.

It was as if everyone who had once filled this space had vanished into thin air, leaving only traces of their existence behind.

"What the hell?" Landon whispered, his voice barely audible, as though speaking too loudly might disturb the invisible force that hung over us. His usual bravado had slipped away, replaced by a fragile vulnerability. He scanned the room, disbelief etched into his features. "This doesn't make any sense."

I picked up a scarf draped carelessly over the back of a plush couch. The fabric was soft and delicate, faintly scented with perfume, as if it had been placed there moments ago by someone who intended to return for it. A chill crept down my spine, raising the hairs on the back of my neck. "It's like they just... walked away."

"Or like they were taken," Jax murmured, stepping closer, his voice laced with a strange fascination. His dark eyes were wide, reflecting an eerie wonder. "This is insane."

Aiden's jaw clenched as he surveyed every corner of the room with his calculating gaze, searching for answers in the chaos. "There has to be an explanation," he insisted, his voice steady but tight with tension. "Maybe they evacuated during an emergency."

I turned to him, my voice trembling slightly as the weight of the situation pressed down on me. "But if that were true, why is everything still here? Why didn't they take their belongings?"

We moved deeper into the ship, the thick silence amplifying the sound of our footsteps. It felt as if the ship itself had swallowed the noise, absorbing everything into its vast, empty halls. The hallways were littered with more luggage—clothes, shoes, even children's toys strewn across the floor, as if their owners had dropped them in a frantic hurry. Each object felt like a snapshot of a life that had abruptly... stopped.

Landon shook his head, his voice dropping to a whisper, unease creeping into every word. "I don't like this," he murmured, the humor that usually colored his tone completely absent. "This place isn't right. We should leave."

"Not yet," Aiden replied, his tone firm but distant, his gaze locked ahead as if piercing through the layers of mystery cloaking the ship. "We need to understand what happened here."

As we pressed further, the atmosphere thickened, an oppressive weight settling around us, like the walls themselves were closing in. We passed by the kitchen, and I froze in my tracks. The scene inside was impossible. Plates of food sat untouched on the counters—steaming dishes, perfectly preserved, as if someone had just finished cooking moments ago. The air was saturated with the rich, savory aroma of freshly prepared meals, hanging eerily in the stillness.

"This can't be real," I whispered, stepping cautiously into the room, my eyes wide with disbelief. I reached out, my fingers trembling as they brushed against one of the plates. The surface was cold, yet the food looked impossibly fresh, too vibrant for a ship that had been abandoned for who knew how long. "This food... it's fresh."

Jax moved beside me, his voice a mix of awe and bewilderment. "How is this even possible?" He glanced around, eyes flickering with excitement despite the tension thickening the air. "This place has been abandoned for... who knows how long."

Aiden stayed silent, his brow deeply furrowed as he surveyed the room. His usual calm had been replaced by something darker, his eyes narrowing as if he was trying to see beyond the surface. He felt it, too—that strange, unnatural force seeping into every corner. "Something's wrong," he said quietly, the finality in his tone sending a chill through the room.

"No kidding," Landon muttered, gripping the edge of the counter so hard his knuckles turned white. His eyes darted nervously around the room, his whole body coiled tight. "I don't know how long this food's been here, but this... this is messed up. None of this is normal."

We stood there for a moment longer, trapped in the surreal perfection of the ship. The untouched food, the absence of life —it felt like we'd stumbled into a story we weren't meant to be a part of. Every instinct screamed to turn back, but it was too late. The deeper we ventured, the more this place demanded to be explored. Something was waiting for us. Something we weren't ready for.

CHAPTER FOUR

SIENNA

"This is incredible!" Jax shouted, his voice echoing through the empty corridors, challenging the thick silence that enveloped us. He held his camera high, capturing every detail with the wide-eyed enthusiasm of someone about to unveil a hidden world. The lens swept across the ship, documenting the eerie stillness as if we were starring in some bizarre reality show. "Can you believe this? It's like we have the whole damn place to ourselves!"

I watched him, amusement mingling with unease, my lips curling into a reluctant smile despite the cold, creeping sensation that had settled deep in my gut since we boarded. Jax's energy was magnetic, a contagious excitement that begged you to dive headfirst into the unknown. Normally, I'd be right there with him, adrenaline pumping and adventure coursing through my veins. But this ship—it felt different from any place we'd explored. A heaviness clung to every corner, every immaculate surface, refusing to let me relax.

Landon, however, embraced the thrill with open arms. Leaning against the railing of the grand staircase, he assumed the role of a tour guide, phone in hand as he narrated his makeshift documentary with exaggerated flair. His voice bounced off the ornate walls, momentarily lightening the oppressive atmosphere around us.

"And here we have the mysterious ballroom!" Landon announced, gesturing theatrically toward the vast, empty space below. "Where ghostly passengers once danced the night away before they mysteriously… vanished!" He wiggled his fingers in mock-spookiness, sarcasm dripping from his tone, unable to suppress his grin.

I laughed, shaking my head at Landon's ridiculousness. He had a knack for making everything feel lighter, less serious— even in situations that screamed the opposite. Right now, his humor was a much-needed buoy, keeping the edges of my anxiety at bay. "You're ridiculous, you know that?"

"Come on, Sienna," he replied, lowering his phone and flashing that familiar grin, his blue eyes twinkling with mischief. "Lighten up! This is exactly why we came here, right? Adventure, mystery, and, if we're lucky, a viral ghost video that catapults us to fame!"

I rolled my eyes but couldn't help smiling. Landon's care-free attitude was like a lifeline, a solid anchor amidst the unsettling stillness that enveloped the ship. His jokes didn't erase the knot in my stomach, but they loosened it just enough to remind me why we were here in the first place.

Ahead, Jax sprinted down the hallway, his footsteps echoing through the vast, empty space with boundless energy. He paused long enough to shoot us an impatient look over his shoulder, his grin unwavering. "Come on, slowpokes! We've got a whole ship to explore!"

Aiden, trailing behind in his usual quiet, thoughtful

manner, stood by the wall, brow furrowed as he traced his fingers along a large, faded map mounted near the elevators. His dark eyes scanned the ship's layout, intense and focused, mentally cataloging every corridor, every room. "This place is massive," he said, his voice low and contemplative. "There's no way we'll cover it all in one night."

I glanced at Aiden, observing how his fingers lingered over the map he had found attached to the wall, tension radiating from him in waves. He wasn't like Jax or Landon—he didn't rush into things without a plan. Aiden needed structure, control, and the assurance that we weren't walking blindly into something we couldn't handle. That need for control was etched all over his face now, his jaw tight as he weighed the risk.

"Then we'd better get moving!" Jax called, practically bouncing in place with excitement. He was already a few steps ahead, his restless energy crackling through the air like static. "Let's split up. We'll cover more ground that way."

I felt Aiden's gaze snap up sharply, his eyes darkening with immediate concern. Splitting up wasn't his style—it went against everything in his nature. He preferred knowing where we all were at any given moment, maintaining structure and predictability. But before he could protest, Landon clapped him on the shoulder with his usual breezy confidence.

"It's fine, Aiden," Landon said, grinning as if we weren't standing in the middle of an empty, ghostly ship with no explanation for its existence. "We're just exploring. What's the worst that could happen?"

Aiden's jaw clenched even tighter, his lips thinning into a straight line as he mulled it over. I could see the conflict in his eyes, the way his instincts battled with the thrill of discovery.

He wanted to keep us safe, to stay in control, but part of him—the adventurer—wanted to uncover the secrets this ship held just as much as the rest of us. That part of him, the one that could never fully resist the pull of the unknown, finally prevailed.

"Fine," Aiden said, his voice low and reluctant. He shot Jax a warning look. "But we stick to the plan. No wandering off too far, and we meet back here in an hour. Got it?"

Jax saluted with mock seriousness, already spinning on his heel and heading toward the next set of hallways. "You got it, boss!"

I exchanged a quick glance with Aiden, feeling the tension still lingering in the air between us. He didn't say anything, but his eyes lingered on mine for a moment longer than usual, as if he was silently telling me to stay close and be careful.

Landon nudged me, that familiar spark of adventure twinkling in his eyes as he leaned in, whispering just loud enough for me to hear, "This is going to be one hell of a story."

I smiled, but something cold pressed down on my chest, a nagging feeling that wouldn't go away. We were here for adventure, for the unknown, but something about this ship felt different. It felt like it was watching us, waiting.

I sensed Aiden's hesitation, but after a beat, he nodded. "Alright. But stay within shouting distance. If anything feels off, we regroup."

With that, we split off into pairs. Aiden and I took one direction, while Landon and Jax headed toward the other end of the ship. The deeper we moved into the heart of the cruise liner, the more surreal everything felt. Signs of life were everywhere—half-packed suitcases in the cabins, fresh linens draped over luxurious four-poster beds, even forgotten cups of coffee sitting on the nightstands, cold but untouched.

The ship seemed suspended in time, as if the passengers had simply stepped away for a moment and never returned. Every detail was unnervingly pristine, from the perfectly arranged furniture to the untouched belongings scattered about. It was like walking through a memory, but one that felt too real, too recent. The air was thick with unsettling quiet, broken only by the faint creak of the ship settling in the water.

Aiden, ever the pragmatist, moved with purpose, methodically checking each door, peeking into rooms, and mapping out the corridors in that sharp mind of his. I could almost see the gears turning behind his calm, focused exterior. His eyes flicked over every detail, searching for answers, for something that would make sense of this impossible place. But he wasn't saying much. The silence between us stretched, heavy and filled with unspoken questions.

I watched him for a moment, the way his hand hovered near the doorframe, his fingers brushing against the metal as if he could feel the weight of the mystery pressing down on him. Aiden was always like this—calm, controlled, trying to solve problems with logic, even when the world refused to offer him any.

"What do you think happened?" I asked, my voice low, almost as if I didn't want to disturb the oppressive stillness that had settled over the ship. It felt like the walls were listening, like the ship itself was holding its breath, waiting for something.

Aiden paused, his hand resting on the edge of a door as he glanced over at me. His dark eyes were intense, calculating, but a shadow of uncertainty lingered there—something I wasn't used to seeing from him. "I don't know," he said finally, his voice thoughtful and measured. "Evacuation, maybe? But if it was an emergency, why leave everything behind? And there's no sign of damage. The ship's completely intact."

I nodded, though his answer didn't bring me any comfort. My fingers trailed absently along the smooth surface of the banister as we descended another set of stairs. The wood felt unnervingly clean and polished, as if it had just been dusted that morning. As we reached the bottom of the staircase, the grand ballroom came into view below us—vast and opulent, with high ceilings and crystal chandeliers hanging overhead like silent sentinels. The room looked untouched by time. In the corner, a grand piano stood with its lid propped open, the keys gleaming under the low light, pristine as if waiting for someone to sit down and play.

"Why would they leave food in the kitchen?" I muttered, more to myself than to Aiden, the question gnawing at me.

Aiden didn't answer immediately. He was lost in thought, his eyes scanning the ballroom, always seeking answers, always trying to piece together a puzzle that had no clear solution. That was the thing about Aiden—he needed explanations. Loose ends bothered him. But this place? It was all loose ends. No matter how hard he tried to apply logic, there was no making sense of the strange stillness surrounding us.

"I think I'm starting to get what you mean," I said, finally breaking the silence between us, though my voice was quieter than before. "This place… it feels weird. Not just empty, but like…"

"Like it's waiting for something," Aiden finished, his voice low, almost a whisper. His gaze remained fixed on the grand ballroom below, his expression unreadable. There was something in the way he said it that sent a chill down my spine. He wasn't the type to jump to conclusions or to succumb to superstitions or paranoia. But here, in this ship frozen in time, even Aiden seemed to feel the weight of something more.

A shiver crawled up my arms, and I rubbed them instinctively, trying to shake off the cold that had crept into my bones. It wasn't the temperature that bothered me—it was the feeling, that gnawing sense that we weren't alone, that the ship was more than just an empty relic. I wanted to laugh it off, to brush it aside like Landon and Jax probably were right now, joking about ghosts and mysteries, but I couldn't. Not here. Not when every inch of this place felt as if it was watching us.

The silence thickened as we moved through the hallways, the echo of our footsteps the only sound. Even though there was nothing—no sign of life, no movement—I couldn't shake the feeling that something, or someone, was there. Watching. Waiting.

After what felt like hours of exploring, weaving through the ship's endless corridors and silent rooms, we finally regrouped near the massive dining hall. The space was grand, filled with towering columns and long, elegant tables stretching beneath dim chandeliers. Landon and Jax were already there, laughing, breathless from whatever excitement they'd uncovered in their section of the ship. Their energy felt at odds with the thick, unsettling silence that hung over everything.

"You wouldn't believe it," Jax said, wiping the sweat from his brow with the back of his hand, his grin wide and unbothered. His dark hair was tousled, and his eyes gleamed with excitement. "We found this luxury suite—fully stocked mini bar and everything. It's like this place is just waiting for people to come back."

Landon leaned against one of the tall, ornately carved chairs, his grin just as infectious. "I was half expecting a butler to show up and offer us a drink." His voice echoed faintly in the vast room, but the playful tone couldn't dispel the strange weight in the air.

I forced a smile, though it felt brittle, the unease inside me growing like a shadow I couldn't quite escape. It had settled in my gut the moment we boarded the ship, and now it felt impossible to ignore. "Maybe we should call it a night. We've seen enough for now."

"Agreed," Aiden said quietly. His tone was clipped, more tense than usual. I glanced over at him and noticed the way his eyes kept darting around the room, scanning the shadows as if he expected something to emerge. He felt it too—the wrongness, the suffocating stillness. Aiden was always calm, always in control, but right now, even he looked unsettled.

Jax waved us off with a casual grin, brushing aside the tension like he didn't feel it. "You guys are too uptight. It's just an old ship. Chill out."

But as we made our way back up to the deck, something had shifted. The silence that had once felt eerie but manageable now weighed heavily, almost suffocating, as if the very air around us had thickened. Every step became harder, as though the ship was pressing down on us, trying to root us in place, to keep us from leaving.

By the time we reached the deck, my heart was pounding in my chest, unease clawing at me from the inside. Something was wrong—I could feel it deep in my bones.

And then I saw it.

Our boat was gone.

I froze, breath rushing from my lungs. My heart slammed against my ribs as panic clawed its way up my throat. "Where's the boat?"

Jax laughed, the sound sharp and disbelieving. He thought it was a joke, his grin still in place but faltering. "Very funny. Where'd you guys tie it off?"

But Aiden didn't answer. He moved toward the edge of the ship, expression hard and focused, jaw clenched. I could see the tension in his movements, the way his eyes narrowed as he scanned the water below. His knuckles turned white as he gripped the railing, face tight with worry.

"It was right here," Aiden said, his voice low and controlled, but I could hear the edge creeping in. "I tied it myself. It shouldn't be gone."

I stepped forward, legs shaky as I made my way to the railing beside him. I leaned over, looking down into the dark, rippling water. The spot where we'd secured the boat was empty, nothing but the endless ocean stretching beneath us. My chest tightened, panic rising faster now, pulse pounding in my ears.

Landon swore under his breath, his earlier humor vanishing in an instant. "There's no way it just... floated off. We secured it. I saw Aiden tie it."

Jax's grin finally dropped, his eyes widening as reality began to settle in. "So, what? It just disappeared?" The disbelief in his voice evaporated, replaced by something far more unsettling—fear. Real, palpable fear.

We stood there, staring at the empty spot where our boat should have been, the cold, hard truth sinking into each of us like a weight. The boat wasn't there. We were stranded. Completely and utterly stranded.

This wasn't fun anymore. We were stuck, and the ship, with its eerie silence and perfect preservation, no longer felt like a mystery waiting to be solved.

It felt like a trap.

And we had walked right into it.

CHAPTER FIVE

SIENNA

The silence was suffocating, pressing in on all sides like the weight of the sea itself. We stood on the deck, eyes locked on the empty expanse of water where our boat had been tethered just an hour ago. The echoes of our laughter and teasing, which had filled the air earlier, vanished as quickly as the boat. A cold, creeping dread slithered through me, twisting in my gut like an illness I couldn't shake. Every beat of my heart seemed louder, reverberating in my chest, an uncomfortable reminder that we were utterly alone.

Aiden was the first to move. His face was hard, jaw clenched tight as he stared down at the dark ocean below, his gaze sharp and unrelenting. His hand gripped the railing so tightly I thought the metal might bend under the pressure. I could see the tension rippling through his body—every muscle locked in that careful way of his, trying to process something that defied explanation.

"It was tied right here," Aiden muttered, his voice barely

audible. He wasn't speaking to us; he seemed more intent on convincing himself. "I tied it. It can't have drifted off."

The words hung in the air, hollow, as if they didn't belong in this thick, unnatural silence.

Jax, for once, wasn't laughing. The usual cocky grin that always seemed plastered on his face had faded, replaced by a tight frown. He ran a hand through his wild hair, fingers raking nervously through the dark strands. "Maybe the rope came loose? Boats do that sometimes, right?" His voice, usually full of bravado, wavered—a clear sign that even he didn't believe what he was saying.

The air felt different now—thick, charged, as if the ship itself had shifted, drawing in a deep breath and holding it. I stepped forward, peering over the railing, my stomach twisting into knots. I kept hoping, wishing, praying I'd look down and see our boat bobbing gently below, that this was all some horrible mistake.

But it wasn't there.

Landon, who always found humor in the darkest situations, stood unusually still beside me, his eyes fixed on the empty horizon. His face, normally animated with jokes and easy smiles, was blank with disbelief. "There's no way," he said quietly, almost a whisper. "No way it just… disappeared."

The words felt heavy, final.

I swallowed hard, trying to keep the rising panic at bay. My voice came out shakier than I wanted. "What do we do?"

Aiden was the calm in the storm, as always. He took a deep breath and straightened, his posture rigid with control, as if sheer willpower could make sense of this chaos. "We find the command room," he said, his voice steady and authoritative.

"If there's a radio, we can signal for help. There has to be something onboard we can use."

No one argued. We clung to Aiden's plan, his certainty, like it was a lifeline. Without it, I wasn't sure how long we could last before the fear swallowed us whole.

We followed him in tense silence as he led us deeper into the ship's cold, echoing belly. What had once felt like an adventure—exploring its vast halls and eerie, untouched rooms—now felt suffocating, as if the walls were closing in with every step. The corridors stretched endlessly, the air colder, biting at my skin. My heart raced as we passed rows of empty cabins, their doors slightly ajar and abandoned luggage strewn across the floors, as if the owners had fled in a hurry. The eerie stillness wrapped around us, thickening with each step we took deeper into the ship's labyrinth.

Jax was the first to break the silence, but even his voice sounded strained, lacking its usual swagger. "This has to be some kind of prank, right?" His eyes darted around, scanning the walls and ceilings, anywhere but at us. "Someone messing with us?"

But no one responded. The truth settled over us, heavy and undeniable.

Landon shook his head. "Who could have done this? There's no one else here."

Jax laughed, but there was no humor in it. "Maybe it's the ghosts."

"Shut up," Aiden snapped, his voice sharp. We all froze for a moment, surprised by the edge in his usually composed demeanor. Aiden never snapped.

"Look," he said more calmly, running a hand through his hair, "we don't know what's going on, but we can't freak out.

We find the command room, get the radio working, and get out of here."

The others nodded, but the unease in the group was palpable. I could feel it too—the way the ship seemed to press in on us. There was a weight in the air, something I couldn't quite explain. It felt alive.

As we navigated through the ship's maze-like corridors, I found myself glancing over my shoulder more often, my nerves buzzing with a growing sense of unease. The shadows at the edge of my vision flickered and danced, but whenever I whipped my head around to look, there was nothing—just empty hallways stretching into the darkness. The silence wasn't just unsettling anymore; it felt alive, pressing in on us from all sides.

"Do you feel that?" I whispered to Aiden, my voice barely audible as we walked side by side. My heart pounded harder with every step, my instincts screaming that something was wrong.

"Feel what?" Aiden's voice was tight, clipped—more focused than afraid, but I could sense the tension there.

I hesitated, unsure how to put the feeling into words. "I don't know. It's like… the ship is watching us."

Aiden didn't respond immediately, but I caught the tightening of his jaw and the flicker of something in his eyes. He felt it too. I knew he did; he just wouldn't say it aloud. Aiden didn't like to give in to fear.

We reached the command room—a large, imposing steel door that groaned as Aiden pushed it open. The sound echoed through the still air, making the hair on the back of my neck stand on end. Inside, the room was cloaked in darkness, save for the faint, eerie glow of emergency lights casting long, ominous shadows across the control panels. Everything looked intact: no signs of damage, no obvious malfunctions. But the silence hung heavy, a weight bearing down on all of us.

Aiden moved immediately to the radio, his movements quick and practiced, the muscles in his forearms flexing as he adjusted dials and flipped switches with precision. He was always calm under pressure, always the problem solver. But with each turn of the dial, his frown deepened, frustration tightening the lines of his face.

"All I'm getting is static," he muttered, his voice low but carrying through the oppressive silence like a warning.

Landon, who had taken up a spot by the window, let out a slow breath. His usual easy-going demeanor was strained, and his attempt at sounding casual fell flat. "Try a different frequency."

Aiden's fingers moved with growing urgency, but he shook his head, frustration seeping through the cracks of his normally calm exterior. "I have. Every channel—it's just static." His voice was harsher now, tinged with disbelief. This wasn't supposed to happen. Not to him. Not with something as simple as a radio.

Jax leaned back against one of the control panels, his posture casual but his eyes betraying the tension thrumming through him, trying to keep things light. "Maybe the radio's just broken," he offered, though a nervous edge crept into his words. "These old ships—stuff doesn't always work."

Aiden shot him a glare, his patience thinning. "It's not broken. It should be working. I don't understand why it isn't." He stared at the controls as if willing them to cooperate, his hands hovering over the dials, looking helpless in a way I had never seen before.

A heavy silence fell over us, the only sound the static hissing from the radio—a noise that seemed to grow louder and more oppressive with each passing second. It filled the room, a white noise amplifying the thick, suffocating tension hanging between us.

"We'll figure something out," Aiden said, breaking the silence, though his voice was firm and determined. He was trying to hold it together—for all of us. "We have to."

Landon, ever the optimist, tried to break the tension, forcing a smile. "Worst case, we start rowing. Who's up for some exercise?" He flashed a grin, but it didn't reach his eyes. There was no humor behind it—just an attempt to keep us from spiraling.

Jax let out a laugh, but it was hollow, his eyes darting between Aiden and the radio. "Yeah, I'm sure we'll paddle back just fine," he said, but his usual bravado was nowhere to be found.

I wanted to laugh with them, to let their jokes soothe the gnawing fear growing steadily in the pit of my stomach. But I couldn't. Something was wrong—terribly wrong. The static from the radio, the bone-chilling cold that seeped into the air, the flickering shadows playing tricks on my mind… it all added up to something I couldn't explain, something darker than I wanted to admit.

"We can't stay here," I blurted, the words spilling from my lips before I realized I'd spoken. My voice trembled, betraying the fear I'd tried to keep hidden.

Aiden turned to look at me, his expression softening for the briefest moment. "We're not staying. I'll figure something out," he promised, but I could hear the uncertainty creeping in —the doubt he was trying to hide.

"No," I said, shaking my head, my arms wrapping around myself as if I could shield against the growing chill in the room. "I mean… this ship. It feels like it's… alive."

Jax raised an eyebrow, his attempt at a cocky grin faltering. "Alive? Like a haunted house kind of deal?" he asked, though the nervous chuckle that followed felt forced.

"I don't know," I whispered, rubbing my arms as if I could shake off the feeling crawling over my skin. "It just… I feel like we're being watched. Like it's waiting for something."

Aiden said nothing, his eyes shifting briefly to the shadows pooling in the corners of the room.

When Aiden's gaze met mine, I caught a flicker of fear in his eyes. He felt it too, but he wouldn't admit it. Not yet.

"We need to keep moving," Aiden said, his voice firm as he straightened his posture, standing taller as if trying to shake off the weight of the situation. His eyes scanned the hallway ahead, determined, though the tightness in his jaw betrayed the strain beneath the surface. "We'll check the lifeboats next. There's got to be something."

We left the command room, the static from the broken radio fading behind us, swallowed by the unsettling quiet of the ship. But the tension remained, thick and suffocating. Every step felt heavier as we moved deeper into the ship's belly. The further we went, the colder the air grew, the chill creeping under my skin like an invisible presence. The walls seemed to hum with a strange energy—a low, barely perceptible vibration crawling through the steel and into my bones.

Every few seconds, I caught glimpses of movement at the edge of my vision—flickers of shadow darting away just as I turned to look. It felt like something was playing with us, staying just out of reach, toying with our nerves. My breath hitched each time, but when I focused, there was nothing. Always nothing.

The walls loomed on either side, narrowing in my mind as if they were closing in, trapping us. Our footsteps echoed in the vast emptiness, amplifying the quiet in a way that made my skin prickle. Each step seemed louder than the last, a reminder that we were alone here, surrounded by silence and the ghosts of something we couldn't see.

My heart raced in my chest, my skin tingling with an undercurrent of fear I couldn't suppress. Panic rose within me, the urge to run clawing at my insides, but I forced myself to stay in control, to keep my steps steady. Running wouldn't change anything. We were stuck here—trapped—and no amount of fleeing would fix that.

"We'll be fine," Jax said from beside me, though his usual swagger was absent. His voice sounded forced, as if he were trying to convince himself as much as the rest of us. "It's just an old ship. Nothing to be scared of."

But even Jax couldn't keep the unease from seeping into his tone. The reckless energy that usually radiated from him had dimmed; his eyes darted around the hallway as if he, too, was seeing things he couldn't explain. His hands were shoved into his pockets, shoulders tense, as if he was bracing for something, even if he wouldn't admit it.

I shot him a look, not bothering to hide my disbelief. He could pretend all he wanted, but none of us were buying it. The bravado, the false sense of calm—it was unraveling. We all felt it. The ship wasn't just a relic of the past; it was alive with something more, something that wasn't going to let us go easily.

CHAPTER SIX

SIENNA

The ship's oppressive silence clung to us like a thick, heavy blanket we couldn't shake off. Each breath felt labored, as if the very air was denser, pressing in on all sides. The deeper we moved through the hallways, retracing our steps from the command room, the more I sensed that something had shifted. The air wasn't just still—it was alive, thick with tension, as if the ship itself were breathing, its pulse intertwined with our own.

"We need to cover more ground," Aiden said, his voice breaking the eerie quiet. His words sliced through the atmosphere, but even his calm, measured tone felt strange now. Aiden always carried himself with control, but the way he stood—rigid, eyes scanning every corner—felt different, as if even he wasn't sure what was going on. "We'll split up. Landon, you take Sienna. Jax, you're with me."

My stomach twisted at the thought of separating. Every instinct screamed against it, but I didn't argue. Aiden always had a plan; he was the anchor that kept us steady. His authority was something we all relied on, but right now, even that comfort felt fragile. The very idea of splitting up made my skin crawl, but we needed answers—and fast.

Landon nudged me, his smirk failing to reach his eyes the way it usually did. "Looks like it's you and me, sunshine. You ready to take on the ghost ship?" His voice was light, but the attempt at humor felt hollow. The tension hanging between us was too thick, too present. Still, I appreciated the effort—Landon, my clown.

I nodded, forcing a smile that didn't quite reach my eyes. "Let's get this over with."

As we split off, Landon and I headed toward the lower decks while Aiden and Jax disappeared up a flight of stairs. The sound of their footsteps faded quickly, leaving an unsettling stillness in their wake. The empty corridor stretched out before us, and I couldn't help but glance over my shoulder. Shadows danced at the edges of my vision, flickering as though they were alive, but when I turned to look, there was nothing—just the eerie stillness that seemed to swallow us whole.

As we walked, the ship groaned around us, the sound deep and guttural, like a beast stirring from its slumber. It felt aware of us, like it was watching, waiting. Each step felt wrong, as if the ship were responding to our presence, shifting beneath our feet with every move we made. My pulse quickened, a growing sense of unease gnawing at the pit of my stomach.

"So, this is officially the creepiest place we've ever been," Landon muttered, his voice echoing in the long, empty hallway. He was trying to keep things light, but there was no mistaking the edge in his tone—he felt it too, the wrongness. "You think we'll find a fully stocked bar down here? Maybe some invisible butlers?"

I let out a weak laugh, more out of obligation than anything else. The tension in my chest was growing with every step. "If we do, you can have the first drink."

The hallways twisted and turned, each one identical to the last, like an endless maze designed to disorient us. It was working. The further we went, the more lost I felt. My heart pounded louder, the sound deafening in my ears as the cold air nipped at my skin. Every corner we turned revealed the same bleak, empty hallway, the dim emergency lights casting long, warped shadows that seemed to follow us like specters.

As we rounded another corner, the lights above us flickered —just for a moment, but enough to send a jolt of fear through me. The shadows stretched longer and darker across the floor, reaching for us.

Then, the door behind us slammed shut with a deafening bang.

I jumped, my breath catching hard in my throat as the sound of the door slamming echoed down the corridor. It was impossibly loud in the stillness, reverberating off the walls as if the ship itself were laughing at us. Landon muttered a curse under his breath, his hand instinctively reaching for my arm. The contact grounded me, even as my heart continued to race.

"It's just the wind," he said, his voice tight and quick. But we both knew there was no breeze here—not this deep into the ship, where the air felt thick and stagnant, where the shadows seemed to have a life of their own.

Still, we kept moving, but each step felt heavier than the last, as if the ship were weighing us down, making it harder to progress. The temperature dropped with every inch we advanced, the chill sinking into my bones, making my skin prickle. My eyes flicked to the mirrors hanging crookedly on the walls—old, cracked, and covered in a fine layer of dust, their once ornate frames now dull with age.

As we passed one, a flicker of movement caught my eye. My breath hitched, and I stopped in my tracks, my heart pounding louder in my ears. Slowly, I turned toward the mirror. For a split second, I could have sworn I saw a face staring back at me—not mine, but a pale, hollow-eyed figure, shrouded in shadow, its gaze piercing and empty.

A sharp gasp escaped me before I could stop it.

"Sienna?" Landon's voice cut through the moment, snapping me back to reality. I blinked, my vision clearing as I stared at my own reflection—wide-eyed and trembling. The figure was gone, replaced by my frightened face.

"N-Nothing," I stammered, tearing my eyes away from the glass and forcing myself to keep moving. "It's nothing."

But I didn't believe it. It didn't feel like nothing. It felt like the ship was toying with me, showing me glimpses of something it wanted me to see—something that shouldn't be there.

The hallway stretched endlessly before us, dimly lit by the flickering emergency lights, each step echoing ominously in the oppressive stillness. Landon kept up his usual string of jokes, but they felt empty now—hollow words meant to fill the growing void of fear. It was as if he were clinging to humor, afraid that acknowledging the truth would only make it worse.

"You know," Landon said, his voice forced and casual, "I bet the ship's just playing tricks on us. Old places like this—they've got history, right? There's probably a ton of explanations for the weird stuff we're seeing. Old pipes, creaky floors…"

I nodded absentmindedly, but my mind wasn't buying it. There was something else lurking here—something malevolent, waiting just beneath the surface. I could feel it in the way the air pressed against my skin, in the way the shadows shifted just outside my line of sight. The ship—whatever it was—wanted us here. It was waiting for something. I couldn't shake the feeling that it wasn't going to let us go.

When we finally reached the dining hall again, the vast room loomed empty and cold, the chandeliers above swaying gently as if disturbed by some invisible force. But there was no breeze; the air was as still and thick as it had been the moment we boarded. Landon glanced around, rubbing the back of his neck nervously. "I don't like this," he muttered, his voice barely audible.

Before I could respond, we heard it—footsteps. At first, they were faint and distant, like they were coming from deep within the ship. But then they grew louder, more distinct, echoing down the hallway behind us. My heart leaped into my throat, and my entire body tensed as a cold dread washed over me.

"Landon…" I whispered, my voice trembling.

"I hear it." His voice was tight now, all traces of bravado gone. We both turned, scanning the empty hallway behind us. But there was no one there—no shadowy figure to match the sound.

Yet the footsteps continued, growing closer, louder—like whoever—or whatever—was making them was right on top of us.

Then, just as suddenly as they had started, the footsteps stopped. Silence rushed back in, thick and suffocating, as if the air had been sucked out of the room.

My blood ran cold. "Let's get back to Aiden and Jax."

Landon didn't argue. We retraced our steps, moving faster

now, our hurried footsteps echoing in the oppressive quiet. The weight of the ship pressed down on us with every turn, the corridors feeling more like a labyrinth designed to trap us than a passageway to safety. By the time we reached the meeting point, I was practically sprinting, my chest tight with the effort to keep my fear at bay.

CHAPTER SEVEN

AIDEN

The cold hit me first as we descended into the lower decks, a biting chill that clung to my skin and seemed to sink deep into my bones. It wasn't just the temperature—something else lingered in the air, gnawing at the edges of my nerves and keeping me on high alert. I tried to concentrate on the task at hand, scanning every corner and shadow, hoping to make sense of what we were witnessing. But nothing about this damn ship made sense anymore.

The crew quarters were unnervingly still, as though time had stopped mid-motion. Some doors stood slightly ajar, offering glimpses into rooms filled with personal belongings, scattered as if abandoned in haste. Open bags, clothes thrown haphazardly across the floor, and half-eaten meals on tables—it was as if the crew had simply vanished, leaving behind the everyday mess of life. Signs of existence were everywhere, yet the absence of people turned those signs into something eerie—something wrong.

The ship groaned beneath us, a low metallic whine echoing in the silence and amplifying the emptiness surrounding us.

Each step we took felt heavier and more deliberate, as if the ship were somehow listening and reacting to our presence. The sensation was almost oppressive, as if we were trespassing in a place we didn't belong. Somewhere we shouldn't be.

I glanced over at Jax, who walked a few paces ahead, his flashlight cutting jagged shadows along the walls. For once, he wasn't saying a word—no jokes, no wisecracks, nothing. Jax's usual method of dealing with tension was to push back, to laugh in the face of fear until everyone else relaxed. But not now. Now, he seemed... wary, his movements stiff with unease. He felt it too—the heaviness, the shift in the air.

"You good?" I asked, keeping my voice low. I had to be the steady one, the one who held it together when things went sideways.

Jax glanced back at me, his face illuminated briefly in the harsh beam of his flashlight. I saw it then—the flicker of doubt in his eyes, something I wasn't used to seeing in him. "Yeah," he replied, his voice quieter than usual. "I just... don't like how this feels, man. We're walking around an empty ship, but it feels like someone's watching us."

I swallowed, my mouth dry. "Yeah," I muttered, the words catching in my throat. "I feel it too."

We lapsed into silence after that, the weight of Jax's words settling between us like a thick fog. He was like me in many ways—always in control, always comfortable pushing the limits but knowing exactly where the line was. But this? This was different. This ship felt like it wanted us here, and we had no idea what we were walking into. That lack of control, that blind uncertainty—it scared him. And it scared me too.

As we rounded a corner, the hallway opened up into a long, narrow passageway. That's when we saw it—a door at the far end of the hall. Unlike the others, which were worn and creaky but otherwise normal, this door was sealed shut, the thick, rusted steel gleaming faintly in the dim light. It didn't belong here. The rest of the ship had been unsettling enough, but this door... it radiated something darker. Something wrong.

Jax stopped, staring at it. "What do you think?" he asked, his voice low and tense, as if he didn't want to disturb whatever was on the other side.

I didn't answer right away. The sight of the door made the hairs on the back of my neck stand up. I didn't like it. The way it seemed to call to us, as though we were being pulled toward it against our better judgment—it felt like the ship was leading us here, like it wanted us to open that door.

"It's different," I finally said, my voice rough. "We should check it out."

I took a step forward, the weight of the decision pressing down on me. But before I could reach it, the door groaned, the rusted metal hinges protesting as it swung open on its own, as if it had been waiting for us.

Jax let out a breath, muttering, "Shit."

He angled the torchlight to shine a beam inside the dark room. The air inside felt heavier, colder, almost suffocating. I could sense it—something was in there, waiting.

I stepped forward cautiously, holding my breath, every instinct screaming at me to turn back. But we had to see. We had to know.

The room inside was small and dark. Jax shined the torch on the walls and flicked on the light switch, which flooded the room with a soft light that flickered occasionally, casting everything in a sickly yellow hue. The walls were covered in photographs. Hundreds of them. Each one pinned haphazardly, some overlapping, some torn at the edges, but all staring at us. Faded, distorted faces, their features twisted and blurred by time and neglect. Some smiled. Others looked terrified. But all of them—every single one—seemed to be watching us, just like the ship.

Passengers. Crew. Maybe people who had come before us —explorers just like us, lost to the ship's grip. I couldn't tear my eyes away from the photographs, each one more haunting than the last.

"What the hell is this?" Jax whispered, his voice trembling slightly.

I didn't have an answer. My mind raced, trying to make sense of it, but the longer I stared, the more I felt it—the ship wasn't just watching us.

It was collecting us.

"What the hell is this?" Jax's voice cut through the suffocating silence.

"I don't know," I muttered, barely above a whisper. But I could feel it—the weight in the air, the pressure bearing down on us from every angle. It wasn't just the photographs lining the walls; there was something alive in this room.

We moved further in, the sound of our footsteps echoing unnaturally loud in the confined space. My eyes swept over the walls and the faces in the photos. They were following us. Every single one of them. I couldn't shake the sensation that the room itself was breathing, feeding off our presence.

"Let's make this quick," I said, my voice tightening with every word. "We need to get back to Sienna and Landon."

Jax was unusually quiet, his focus drawn to one of the photographs pinned near the door. His face was tense, his usual cocky grin replaced with something far darker. "You think these were the people... the ones who disappeared?"

I didn't answer, because I didn't need to. We both knew what this was. These photos were remnants of lives that had been snatched away. These people—they weren't here anymore. The unspoken truth lingered between us: if we didn't get off this ship soon, we'd end up just like them.

Before I could say anything else, the door behind us slammed shut with a force that rattled the walls. The sound was a violent crash, as if the ship was sealing us in. My heart leapt into my throat as I spun around, my pulse roaring in my ears.

"What the—" Jax was at the door in an instant, yanking at the handle. "It's locked!"

A cold wave of dread washed over me, sinking into my skin and settling in my bones. My chest tightened as I rushed to Jax's side, pulling on the door with him. "Jax, help me get this open."

We pulled and yanked, but it wouldn't budge. The air around us grew colder, a sharp bite that made my breath visible in the dim light. I could feel it in my gut—something was wrong. Something far worse than we'd expected.

And then the whispers started.

Low at first, like the wind—unintelligible and far away. But then they grew louder, closer, until they swirled around us like a storm. The voices pressed in from all sides, overwhelming. I clamped my hands over my ears, trying to block them out, but it didn't matter. They weren't just in the room—they were inside us, tearing through my mind, making it impossible to think.

"Aiden!" Jax's shout barely broke through the chaos. "What the hell is happening?"

"I don't know!" I yelled back, though deep down, I did know. The ship wasn't empty. It had never been empty. It was alive.

Suddenly, Jax was ripped from his feet by an unseen force, flung across the room like a ragdoll. He slammed into the wall with a sickening crack that echoed through the claustrophobic space. My stomach twisted as he crumpled to the floor, motionless, the sharp sound of impact still ringing in my ears.

"Jax!" I shouted, my heart pounding as I rushed toward him, my pulse hammering in my throat. He lay there, limp, his face pale with blood trickling from the corner of his mouth. His eyes were closed, his chest barely rising and falling. Panic seized my chest as I pressed my fingers to his neck, searching for a pulse. It was there—faint, but steady.

"We need to get out of here," I muttered, my voice trembling as dread washed over me in waves. But the words felt small and useless against the horror unfolding. The room was closing in, the walls vibrating with a dark energy that made it hard to breathe. The air around us thickened with something alive—something angry.

The whispers rose again—low and unintelligible at first, swirling through the room like a dark wind. But they quickly grew louder, more insistent, until they became an ear-splitting wail that seemed to echo from everywhere at once. I clamped my hands over my ears, but it didn't help. The voices weren't just around us—they were inside us, tearing through my mind, making it impossible to think.

"Come on, Jax, wake up!" I shouted, shaking his shoulder,

desperate to rouse him, but he didn't stir. His body felt too heavy, too still, and the air grew colder by the second.

I glanced around wildly, desperate for a way out. The door. I sprinted toward it, throwing my body against it, yanking at the handle. It wouldn't budge. "No, no, no!" I muttered, pulling with all my strength. "Come on, damn it, open!"

The room shook, the whispers morphing into blood-curdling screeches. The photographs rattled violently on the walls, as if they might tear themselves free and fly at us. The walls closed in, threatening to swallow us whole.

"Jax, help me!" I shouted over the chaos, but he remained unresponsive. The ship's weight pressed down on me, determined to keep us trapped, to bury us beneath its haunting secrets.

Finally, with a groaning creak, the door flew open, crashing against the wall. I seized Jax by the arms, dragging him out with every ounce of strength I had left. The moment we crossed the threshold, the door slammed shut behind us, sealing the horrors inside. The whispers ceased, the screams cut off abruptly, leaving us in eerie silence. Yet the oppressive weight of the ship lingered, looming over us like a dark, malevolent presence.

I collapsed in the hallway, gasping for breath, Jax's limp body beside me. His breathing was shallow, his face ashen. My chest tightened painfully at the sight of him—this wasn't the Jax I knew. He had always been so full of life, so unshakable. Now, he lay there, barely hanging on.

I peered down the corridor, my mind racing. We were utterly alone—no Sienna, no Landon to help us. Just me and Jax, trapped in the belly of a ship that didn't want us to leave. We needed to find the lifeboats, and fast.

Jax groaned softly, his eyes fluttering open for a fleeting moment before closing again. I pressed my hand to his forehead, feeling the clammy chill of his skin. He needed medical attention—immediately. But we were so far from any help, and the ship… the ship wasn't going to let us go easily.

"Hang in there, Jax," I whispered, my voice hoarse and shaky. "I'm getting us out of here."

Yet, even as the words left my lips, a cold, terrifying thought took root in the back of my mind: I had no idea how to escape. I didn't know if we could escape.

CHAPTER EIGHT

SIENNA

Aiden's voice shattered the heavy silence like a blade slicing through thick fog. "Sienna! Landon!" His shout ricocheted off the cold metal walls, each syllable reverberating down the endless corridors, making the entire ship shudder with his urgency. My heart lurched into my throat, and without thinking, I grabbed Landon's arm, my grip tight with panic.

"Did you hear that?" I whispered, my voice trembling. It felt as if the air around us had thickened, each breath becoming a struggle.

Landon's expression darkened, his face taut with a mix of fear and frustration. He didn't need to say anything; the tension radiating off him was palpable. "Yeah," he muttered, already moving before I could react. "We need to go. Now."

We sprinted down the narrow hallway, our footsteps a frantic rhythm against the creaking floor, the oppressive atmosphere of the ship closing in with every step. The flickering lights above cast long, distorted shadows that danced along the walls, their erratic buzzing making my skin crawl. It felt as if the ship itself was alive—pulsing, breathing, watching us—and the deeper we went, the more I sensed its presence.

It was waiting.

"Come on, Sienna!" Landon's voice was taut, barely containing the rising panic that crackled in the air. He tugged me along, his grip firm, but I could sense the same dread gnawing at him, threatening to unravel us both. "We don't have time."

We rounded a corner, and the sight that met us hit like a punch to the gut. Aiden knelt beside Jax, who lay crumpled on the floor, his body eerily still. Blood streaked down the side of Jax's face, a deep crimson stain against his pale skin, draining him of the vibrant energy I knew so well. His eyes fluttered open, but they were unfocused, dazed. He looked like a ghost of himself—fragile, broken.

I froze, my stomach twisting into knots. "Aiden, what happened?" My voice trembled as I dropped to my knees beside Jax. My hands hovered over him, shaking and unsure of where to start. Panic seized me as I glanced at Landon, whose breath came in shallow, ragged bursts, his eyes wide with terror.

Aiden rose to his feet, wiping a hand across his forehead, his face pale beneath the dim, flickering lights. Sweat clung to his skin, and his jaw was clenched so tightly that I feared it might shatter. "Something threw him across the room," he said, his voice strained, barely above a whisper. His eyes flicked between us—desperate but striving to remain composed. "I don't know what it was, but we need to patch him up. Fast."

Landon's face contorted, his hands clenching into fists at

his sides. The usual cocky glint in his eyes was gone, replaced by a raw, unfiltered fear I had never witnessed before. "We need to get off this ship. Now," he snapped, his voice trembling with barely restrained panic. "This place—it's trying to kill us."

I could feel his fear radiating toward me, the same terror I was desperately trying to suppress. But I couldn't deny the truth in his words. Something was profoundly wrong. Horribly wrong. And the ship wasn't going to let us leave easily.

We had to stay focused. Jax was still bleeding, still fading fast. We couldn't afford to fall apart—not yet.

"We'll figure it out," I said, forcing my voice to steady as I placed a hand on Landon's arm, trying to ground him, to prevent him from spiraling further. "But first, we need to help Jax. Please."

Landon's gaze met mine, wild and conflicted, but after a moment, he exhaled sharply and nodded. His fists slowly relaxed, but the tension remained coiled in his shoulders. "Fine. But we can't stay here long. This place… it's doing something to us."

He wasn't wrong. Even as we stood there, the air around us pressed in tighter, heavier, the ship's malevolent force wrapping around us like a suffocating shroud. I felt it in my bones —the ship was awake, and it was hungry.

Aiden's eyes hardened as he took charge again, his voice clear and resolute. "We need to find a med room to patch Jax up. Then we figure out how the hell we're getting off this thing."

Without another word, we hoisted Jax between us and plunged down the hallway, deeper into the belly of the ship.

Every step felt like a descent into something darker, far more dangerous than we'd ever imagined.

And somehow, I knew it wasn't going to let us leave without a fight.

Landon's eyes were wild, frantic, as he practically shouted, "We're wasting time! We need to find a lifeboat—anything to get us the hell off this ship!"

His entire body trembled, anger and fear bubbling over, barely contained. I could feel the panic radiating from him like a tidal wave, and it took every ounce of my strength to remain calm.

"Landon, we will," I said softly, forcing my voice to steady, even as my own fear clawed at my insides. "But we have to take care of Jax first. He needs us." My words hung between us, heavy with unspoken urgency.

Landon's eyes locked onto mine, wide with desperation, his chest heaving as he fought for control. For a moment, it seemed like he would argue, like his panic might swallow him whole. But then, slowly, he drew a deep breath. His shoulders sagged slightly, the fight fading from him as he nodded, almost reluctantly. "Fine," he muttered, his voice rough and edged with a fear that wouldn't dissipate. "But we can't stay long."

Aiden was already stepping up to take charge again. "Let's go. There's got to be a med room somewhere on this ship."

We moved as one, the four of us navigating the ship's twisted, labyrinthine hallways. Jax was barely conscious, his weight resting heavily between Aiden and me as we struggled to support him. Every few steps, he groaned in pain, his head lolling forward, his face pale and slick with sweat. His injuries were severe—worse than I wanted to admit—but he was still with us. Barely.

The deeper we ventured into the ship's bowels, the more it felt alive around us. Doors that had once been firmly closed now stood wide open, gaping like dark mouths eager to swallow us whole, while others that had been passable were suddenly sealed tight, locking us in. The lights flickered overhead, casting eerie, shifting shadows that heightened our disorientation. It was as if the ship itself were shifting beneath our feet, altering its form, trying to ensnare us.

Then, as we passed a narrow, dimly lit hallway, I froze. Sienna. A voice—soft, distant, and unmistakable—whispered my name. It felt like it was carried on the wind, but there was no wind down here. I turned, my heart slamming against my ribs as I strained to hear it again.

"Did you hear that?" I asked, my voice barely more than a whisper.

Aiden glanced at me, his brow furrowed in confusion. "Hear what?"

I swallowed hard, my mouth suddenly dry. "Someone… someone called my name." The words felt strange on my tongue, as if I couldn't quite accept them even as I spoke.

Landon was already ahead, not bothering to look back. "We don't have time for this, Sienna," he snapped, his voice tight with tension, each hurried step betraying his own rising fear.

I hesitated, staring down the darkened corridor, my pulse pounding in my ears. It hadn't been my imagination. I felt it. The ship was speaking to me. A cold, dark certainty settled over me like a shroud. The connection pulsed in my bones, whispering in my mind. I couldn't explain it, but it was undeniable. The ship wasn't just haunting us—it was calling to me.

I forced myself to move, shoving the feeling deep down as

we continued onward. But it lingered, gnawing at the edges of my consciousness, refusing to let go.

After what felt like an eternity, we finally found what we were searching for—a small, sterile medical room tucked away in the lower levels. It seemed almost untouched by time, the sharp smell of antiseptic lingering in the air, unsettling in its starkness.

We laid Jax down on the cold, metal table, his body limp and unresponsive. My hands trembled as I rifled through the cabinets, searching for anything that might help. Gauze, antiseptic wipes, painkillers—I snatched everything within reach, my breath coming in quick, shallow gasps. Aiden worked alongside me, his movements swift and precise, yet the strain on his face was unmistakable. His calm facade was fracturing, piece by piece.

"We're gonna fix you up, man," Aiden murmured to Jax, though the words lacked the usual conviction he carried. Jax stirred, his eyes fluttering open for a brief moment before drifting shut again. His breaths were shallow, his skin clammy and pallid.

Landon was a bundle of restless energy, pacing near the door, fingers twitching anxiously at his sides. He was taut with nervous energy, glancing toward the hallway every few seconds as if expecting something to emerge from the shadows. "This is insane," he muttered, mostly to himself. "We need to leave—right now." His voice wavered with the raw panic he fought to suppress. "This ship's alive. It's playing with us."

Aiden glanced up from where he was tending to Jax's wounds, his eyes narrowing with determination. "We'll get out of here," he said firmly. "But Jax needs time to rest, and we need to figure out how to reach the lifeboats without getting ourselves killed."

Landon scoffed but offered no argument. Instead, he continued pacing, his head snapping toward every creak and groan of the ship. He was unraveling, and I couldn't blame him. The weight of the ship's malevolence pressed down on all of us, thick and suffocating.

The lights flickered again, this time longer, plunging us into total darkness for several heart-stopping seconds before buzzing back to life. In that moment of blackness, the feeling returned—stronger, more insistent. The ship was focusing on me. Watching me. Waiting for me.

My breath hitched as I glanced toward the door, my pulse racing in my ears. And then I heard it again—clearer this time, a whisper right at my ear. Sienna.

I shivered, wrapping my arms around myself as if that could shield me from the cold grip of the ship. The others hadn't heard it, but I had. I couldn't deny it any longer. The ship was singling me out, drawing me in, and with every passing second, its hold on me grew tighter.

Jax stirred, a faint groan escaping his lips as his eyelids fluttered. For a moment, he seemed trapped in the haze of unconsciousness, his brow furrowing as though he were struggling to pull himself back to reality. His chest rose and fell more steadily now, but he was still pale, his face slick with cold sweat. Slowly, his eyes cracked open, dazed and unfocused, blinking as if the dim, flickering lights were too bright.

"Jax," I whispered, leaning closer, relief flooding through me like a warm tide. "You're awake."

He blinked slowly, his gaze sharpening with each passing second, confusion giving way to something far more unsettling

—fear. His hands twitched at his sides, and he attempted to push himself up, only to falter, his strength failing him. His head lolled to the side, a grimace of pain twisting his features.

Aiden moved quickly, steadying him with a hand on Jax's shoulder. "Easy, man. Don't push it. You're still hurt."

Jax groaned, his voice rough and thick, as if speaking were an effort that pained him. "We need to get out of here," he rasped, urgency slicing through the grogginess that still clouded his mind. His eyes darted nervously around the room, as if expecting something to lunge at us from the shadows. "This place... it's not right."

His words sent a chill racing down my spine. Jax, the one who was always the first to dive headfirst into danger, was scared. Truly scared. The bravado and reckless confidence that usually defined him had vanished, replaced by a vulnerability I had never witnessed before.

Aiden's grip tightened on Jax's shoulder, his voice a steady anchor. "We will, I promise. Just hang in there, okay? We'll get you out."

But I could see it—the cracks forming in Aiden's resolve. He fought to stay in control, to keep us grounded, yet the weight of the situation bore down on him, responsibility gnawing at him like a relentless predator. His eyes, usually sharp and clear, were clouded with exhaustion and worry.

Landon, who had been pacing relentlessly near the door, abruptly stopped, fists clenched tightly at his sides. "We shouldn't be hanging around!" he snapped, his voice sharp with frustration and fear. "This place is messing with us, and you all know it." Tremors coursed through him, his fear finally getting the better of him, pushing him closer to the edge.

I forced myself to focus on Jax, whose eyes fluttered

closed again, his breaths shallow and ragged. "Jax, stay with me," I urged softly, brushing my fingers gently along his arm. "We're not leaving you."

He struggled to open his eyes again, the effort evident in every strained movement. When he met my gaze, his voice emerged a little stronger, yet thick with exhaustion. "Sienna… we can't stay here. I've never felt anything like this." He paused, sucking in a shaky breath. "I thought... I thought I was dying."

His words struck me like a punch to the gut, tightening my chest painfully. I glanced at Aiden, whose jaw was clenched so tightly I feared it might shatter. Landon had fallen silent, standing stiffly near the door, refusing to meet our eyes. He didn't need to voice it—we were all thinking the same thing. This ship wasn't just a bad place. It was alive, and it craved something from us. From me.

"We'll find a way off this ship," Aiden repeated, this time more to himself than to Jax. He fought to maintain control, but the strain was starting to show on his face. The ship's hold on us grew stronger by the minute.

I looked at them—Jax, brought to his knees by whatever malevolent force was at play; Aiden, barely holding it together; and Landon, whose fear had stripped him of his usual humor and confidence. The ship was tearing us apart, piece by piece, and I didn't know how much longer we could endure.

Jax shuddered, trembling as he leaned back against the table, his eyes fluttering closed again. "I'm telling you," he muttered, his voice barely a whisper, "we need to get out. Before it takes one of us."

Aiden's jaw tightened, but he nodded, his gaze flicking to the door as if calculating every possible escape route in his mind. "We will," he said, though the conviction in his voice wavered like a flickering candle.

Yet even as he spoke, I sensed the truth beneath his words. This ship—it wasn't going to let us go easily. Its claws were deep in us now, and with each passing moment, its grip tightened.

CHAPTER NINE

JAX

The medical room felt like a freezer, the cold biting deeper with each passing second, creeping under my skin and settling into my bones. Every breath I took sent sharp stabs of pain through my ribs, each inhale a painful reminder of how close I had come to death. The weight of it all —this ship, this nightmare—made me feel small and useless. I hated being sidelined, forced to sit here while Aiden and Sienna worked to find a way off this floating death trap. The walls seemed to close in on me, the oppressive silence gnawing at my nerves.

Landon sat across from me, perched on the edge of a chair, his body relaxed but his eyes telling a different story. He always carried himself with that easygoing, cocky charm, even when everything was falling apart around him. His faint grin tugged at his lips, as if he were trying to maintain some semblance of normalcy for both of us. But I could see it—the tension in his eyes, the way his fingers tapped impatiently against his knee. No one was fooling anyone; the strain was getting to all of us.

"So," Landon finally said, his voice cutting through the cold, "think when we get off this haunted piece of shit, Sienna's finally gonna give in and let you have that baby you're always pestering her about?"

His tone was casual and light, as if we were lounging on the deck of our boat instead of trapped inside a medical room that felt like it was closing in on us. I managed a laugh, though it came out as more of a wheeze, the pain in my chest flaring up in protest.

"Keep dreaming," I said, wincing. "You know Sienna. Stubborn as hell. It'll take more than a ship trying to kill us to change her mind."

Landon leaned back in his chair, crossing his arms over his chest, that grin of his widening just enough to show he wasn't giving up. "Nah, man. She'll definitely give in. Plus, that baby's gonna be mine—strongest swimmers, best genes. Kid's gonna come out looking just like me. Handsome as shit."

His confidence, his ability to joke even now, made me smile despite everything. That was Landon—always finding a way to lighten the darkest situations, as if he could laugh away the fear. "Yeah, right. That baby's gonna have a mouth like mine and a temper like Sienna's. We'll be in trouble."

His laughter filled the room, the sound bouncing off the cold metal walls. For a brief moment, it felt like we were back to normal—just two friends talking crap, making plans for a future we weren't even sure we'd see. The warmth of his laugh was familiar, a lifeline in the middle of the storm.

But just as quickly as it had come, it vanished.

The temperature in the room dropped so fast it felt like someone had flipped a switch. The warmth was ripped away, leaving nothing but biting cold in its place. It wasn't natural. It wasn't right. The chill wrapping around us wasn't just from the air; it crept deeper, gnawing at my chest and quickening my heartbeat with a sudden, inexplicable fear.

Landon's grin faltered, his eyes narrowing as he turned toward the door. "Did you feel that?"

I nodded, instinctively sitting up straighter, my muscles tensing. "Yeah. I feel it."

The air in the room felt thick now, heavy with an oppressive weight that pressed down from every angle. I glanced at the door, half-expecting to see something lurking in the shadows, but there was only eerie stillness and biting cold.

Landon's easygoing demeanor shifted; his body stiffened as if he sensed the wrongness too. Doubt flickered in his eyes —an expression I wasn't used to seeing on him. For a moment, we sat in silence, listening, waiting.

The temperature dropped even further, the cold so intense that my breath fogged in front of me. The lights overhead flickered once, twice, casting long, jagged shadows across the room. I forced myself to breathe, struggling to suppress the rising panic that threatened to take over.

"Landon…" I began, my voice low and shaky.

But before I could continue, a deep, guttural rumble began. It resonated in the walls, vibrating through the metal, crawling up my spine like icy fingers. The ship groaned as if something deep inside it was awakening. The hair on the back of my neck prickled, and a cold sweat broke out across my skin.

Landon stood slowly, his eyes fixed on the doorway. "What the hell is that?"

I swallowed hard, dread tightening around my chest. "I don't know."

But I knew, deep down, this was no ordinary ship creak. This was something else—something far worse.

And it was coming for us.

The low, guttural sound erupted, a deep rumble resonating from the very heart of the ship. It vibrated through the walls and the floor, crawling up my spine like an icy hand. The lights flickered above us, casting long, distorted shadows that twisted and danced across the room. My heart raced, every instinct screaming at me to run, but I was frozen, ensnared by an overwhelming sense of dread.

"Landon…" I whispered, but my words were swallowed by the suffocating shift in the atmosphere. The air thickened, as if the ship itself had taken a deep breath, and everything felt unnaturally tilted, off-balance.

Landon's body jerked violently, his muscles spasming, eyes snapping wide open with terror. Before I could react, he was lifted off the ground, feet dangling, arms flailing as if something unseen had seized him. He hung there, suspended like a broken marionette, limbs twitching in ways they shouldn't. His mouth opened in a silent scream, eyes bulging with agony and fear. The room, already frigid, felt like it dropped another ten degrees, the walls groaning as if in pain.

"No!" I shouted, the sound tearing from my throat as I fought to push myself up. My ribs screamed in protest, pain shooting through my side, but I didn't care. I had to get to him. I had to stop whatever was happening. But something held me back—an invisible force pressing against my chest, weighing me down like a leaden blanket.

Landon's body contorted, bones cracking with sickening pops as his limbs twisted at unnatural angles. The sound was unbearable, his grotesque transformation like a scene from a nightmare. Our eyes met for the briefest moment, wide with terror, pleading. In that instant, I saw it—the raw, helpless fear reflected back at me. He knew he wasn't getting out of this.

Then, as if the ship had decided it was finished with him, Landon was hurled across the room with brutal, unrelenting force. The sickening crunch of his body hitting the wall made my stomach lurch. He crumpled to the ground, his form folding in on itself, broken and limp, like a discarded rag doll.

"Landon!" I screamed, my voice cracking with panic. I pushed off the bed, the invisible force lifting, and stumbled forward, ignoring the sharp pain tearing through my ribs. But before I could reach him, a violent gust of wind sucked his body out of the room, as if the ship had swallowed him whole. The door slammed shut behind him with a deafening bang, the sound echoing in the suffocating silence that followed.

Breath coming in short, ragged gasps, my heart pounded so hard I thought it might burst. I yanked the door open, the cold metal biting into my fingers as I staggered into the hallway, my mind swirling in panic and disbelief.

And there he was.

Landon lay crumpled in the middle of the corridor, his limbs twisted in ways no human body should ever bend. His neck was bent at an unnatural angle, his head lolling to the side. His eyes—once so full of life and laughter—stared blankly at the ceiling, devoid of everything that had made Landon who he was.

"No, no, no," I muttered, my voice barely more than a broken whisper as I collapsed beside him. My hands hovered over his body, trembling and too afraid to touch him. What if I touched him and he shattered? What if I touched him and it made this all real?

Landon was gone.

I didn't hear the pounding footsteps echoing down the hallway until Sienna's voice cut through the haze like a knife, sharp and panicked. "Jax! What—" Her words faltered, dying in her throat as her eyes landed on Landon's body.

Her face went ghost-white, the blood draining from her cheeks in an instant. "No," she whispered, her voice breaking as she dropped to her knees beside him. "No, no, no." Her hands reached for him, trembling as she cradled his face, her fingers smoothing back his hair as if that simple act could bring him back.

"Landon, please." Her voice cracked, tears streaming down her face as she rocked back and forth, clutching him to her chest. "Please wake up. I love you. Please don't leave me."

She kept whispering, over and over, each word stabbing through me like a knife. I couldn't move. I couldn't speak. All I could do was watch as Sienna's heart shattered in front of me, her sobs filling the empty, echoing hallway.

Aiden was there too, standing just behind her, his face pale and drawn tight with pain. His jaw was clenched, the tension in his body barely contained, but his eyes... his eyes told the truth. He was scared. We all were.

I saw it—the brutal reality sinking into his gaze: Landon was gone, and this ship was just beginning. We weren't safe. We never were.

But Sienna—she couldn't stop. She couldn't let go of Landon, her sobs growing louder and more desperate. "We need you," she whispered through her tears, clutching his lifeless hand to her chest. "We're not the same without you."

Aiden stepped forward, gently placing his hand on Sienna's shoulder, trying to pull her away, but she resisted, gripping

Landon's face as if she could will him back to life. For a moment, I thought she might rip herself apart trying to hold on to him.

"Come on, Sienna," Aiden said, his voice soft but urgent. "We have to keep moving."

But how could we move? How could any of us move when Landon—our friend, our family—lay dead in front of us?

The lights overhead flickered again, casting long, eerie shadows down the hallway. The ship groaned, as if satisfied with its first victim and already hungry for more.

I looked down at Landon's still body, the laughter that used to fill my life now gone, replaced by this suffocating silence. My heart felt as if it were being crushed under the weight of it all, and I wasn't sure I could take it.

I wasn't sure any of us could.

We had been a group—a team, a family. Now, we were just pieces, broken and scattered, trying to survive something we couldn't understand.

Landon was dead. And if the ship had its way, we'd be next.

We weren't getting out of this.

Landon's body lay still on the cold floor, his face peaceful despite the violence that had taken him. The ship had claimed its first victim, but it wouldn't be the last.

Sienna's sobs filled the corridor, her hands gripping Landon's face as if she could will him back to life. "We need you," she whispered, her voice breaking. "We're not the same without you."

I wanted to say something to comfort her, but the words wouldn't come. My mind was a haze of disbelief and horror, my body shaking uncontrollably. Landon was gone. He was really gone. And the ship… it wasn't finished with us.

Aiden finally stepped forward again, his hand resting on Sienna's shoulder as he gently pulled her away from Landon's body. She resisted at first, her fingers clutching desperately to him, but eventually, she let go, collapsing into Aiden's arms. He held her, his face tight with grief, but his eyes… his eyes were hard now, the realization of what we were up against settling in.

The ship wasn't just a place; it was alive, and it wanted us.

I wasn't sure I could handle this. I wasn't sure any of us could.

But I knew one thing for sure:

We were next.

CHAPTER TEN

SIENNA

The cold wasn't just in the air anymore—it was inside me. It felt as if the ship had sunk its icy claws into my skin, chilling me from the inside out. My hands wouldn't stop shaking, the tremors a cruel reminder of how long I had held onto Landon, begging him to wake up, to be okay. But he hadn't moved. His eyes hadn't fluttered open with that lazy, playful grin of his. He hadn't teased me with some offhand joke. He was gone. And now, it was just the three of us.

I sat on the floor, my back pressed against the wall, staring at his lifeless body. I couldn't move. It was as if all the energy had drained out of me, leaving only the crushing weight of grief and disbelief. The air felt heavy, pressing down on us, suffocating in its oppressive stillness. The silence that lingered in the room was the kind you only felt after something truly terrible had happened—a silence that screamed louder than any words ever could.

Aiden stood a few feet away now, his posture stiff, fists

clenched at his sides. His face was pale, his jaw set tight, as if he were holding everything inside by sheer force of will. He wasn't looking at me. He wasn't looking at Jax. He just stared down the corridor, his mind somewhere far away, desperately trying to hold the pieces together.

Jax, however, was anything but still. He paced like a caged animal, his footsteps erratic and loud in the small room, each step more frantic than the last. His breathing was shallow and ragged, his chest rising and falling too fast. I could see the tremble in his hands, the way his fingers twitched at his sides, unable to stay still. He was like a tightly coiled spring, ready to snap at any moment.

"We need to get the hell off this ship," Jax muttered, his voice barely above a growl, thick with desperation. He stopped pacing for a moment, his eyes locking onto Landon's body, his expression a mixture of horror and disbelief. "Before it takes us all."

Aiden finally tore his gaze away from the hallway and looked at Jax. His eyes were hard, filled with a determination that felt forced, as if he were clinging to some shred of control that was slipping away with every second. "We're not getting off this ship if we lose our heads."

Jax let out a bitter, humorless laugh, shaking his head as if Aiden had said something ridiculous. His voice rose, the panic bubbling up, threatening to spill over. "Lose our heads? Landon is dead, Aiden. This ship killed him. What's next, huh? You? Sienna? Me?" His words were sharp, cutting through the room like shards of glass. "You really think staying calm is going to save us? We're trapped! It's hunting us, and you're acting like we can just outsmart it!"

Aiden's jaw tightened, the muscles in his neck flexing as

he tried to stay composed. His calm demeanor was hanging by a thread, and I could see it fraying. "We need a plan," he said slowly, forcing the words through clenched teeth. "We can't just run around, Jax. We need to find a way to communicate with the outside world. Maybe there's still a working radio—something. We can't give up."

But Jax wasn't hearing it. His wild eyes darted between Aiden and me, as if we were the ones who had lost our minds. Fear and rage swirled inside him, mixing into something dangerous, something volatile. He stepped closer to Aiden, his fists clenching so tightly that his knuckles turned white.

"There's no plan, Aiden," Jax spat, his voice shaking with fury. "This thing—whatever it is—isn't going to let us go. It wants us dead. And the longer we stay, the more we're feeding it."

I watched them, my heart pounding in my chest, desperate to find the right words to break the tension. But I had nothing. What could I say? Jax wasn't wrong. The ship wanted us dead. We had felt it from the moment we set foot on this cursed vessel. It was as if the ship had its own malevolent will, its own twisted consciousness, playing with us—waiting for the perfect moment to snuff us out one by one.

"We're not giving up," Aiden said, his voice sharp and commanding. He stepped toward Jax, his eyes dark, filled with a fire I hadn't seen in him before. "We're getting off this ship, but not if we lose it first. We need to keep our heads on straight."

Jax's face twisted in anger, breath coming in harsh, shallow gasps. "Landon is gone, Aiden! We're all next—don't you get that? There's no plan that's going to save us!"

I stood, my legs shaky, still trembling from the aftershock

of everything. I placed a hand on Jax's arm, trying to calm him, even though I wasn't sure I believed what I was about to say. "We need each other, Jax. We can't survive this if we're at each other's throats."

He looked at me, his eyes softening just slightly, but the fear in them was raw, barely contained. His body was tense, vibrating with energy that had nowhere to go. "Sienna, I can't lose you too," he said, voice cracking with emotion. "I can't."

"You won't," I whispered, my voice trembling. "But we need to stay focused. We have to keep moving."

For a moment, the tension in the room held thick and suffocating. Then Jax let out a shaky breath and stepped back, running a hand through his hair, fingers trembling. "Fine," he muttered. "But if this thing tries to take one more of us…"

"It won't," Aiden repeated, but even he seemed to be grasping at the words, trying to convince himself as much as us. His face, usually composed, was tight, the strain in his eyes betraying the calm he desperately clung to. The truth lingered in the air between us—unspoken yet heavy: we were all terrified. None of us knew what to believe anymore.

Landon's body lay cold and still on the floor, a silent reminder of how little time we had left. My gaze flickered to him, to the man who had been our anchor through every insane thing we'd survived together. But he was gone. The warm, joking spark in his eyes had been snuffed out. I swallowed hard, trying to push back the grief, but it was like holding back the tide.

We had to move. Now.

"Jax, please," I whispered, my voice barely audible, yet it was all the strength I could muster. "We need to stick together. We can't let it tear us apart."

Jax turned to me, and for a moment, I saw the real Jax—the one who always had a quick grin or a laugh at the ready. His expression softened, his eyes meeting mine with a flicker of vulnerability, but beneath that lay something darker: fear. It wasn't just creeping up on him anymore; it was overtaking him, weaving into every movement.

"Sienna, you know I'm right," he said, his voice tight and strained. His hand twitched at his side, fingers flexing as if he were fighting the urge to hit something again. "You've felt it, haven't you? This ship… it's in our heads. It's twisting every-thing, making us weak."

I had felt it. That sickening pull, like something crawling under my skin. The shadows seemed to whisper my name, taunting me. I could feel the ship watching us, feeding off our fear, growing stronger with every passing second. But I couldn't give in to that—not now. Not when we were all we had left.

"We're not moving without a plan," Aiden interjected, his voice firm, though his gaze remained locked on Jax, as if he were waiting for him to explode. "We're going to get through this, but we can't start turning on each other. That's exactly what it wants."

Jax let out a bitter laugh, the sound raw and jagged, like it had been ripped from his throat. He turned to face Aiden fully, his body trembling with barely contained rage. "What it wants?!" His voice cracked, the anger giving way to something far more broken. "Landon is dead, Aiden! What more does it want from us?!"

Aiden took a deep breath, his control hanging by a thread. "I know," he said, his voice quieter now, almost pleading. "I know, Jax. But we need to stay focused. We can't fall apart now. We can't let it win."

But I could see it—the cracks forming in all of us. The ship wasn't just killing us physically; it was tearing us apart from the inside, piece by piece, feeding on our fear, grief, and anger. And Jax… Jax was already starting to unravel.

"I'm not sitting here waiting to die," he muttered, shaking his head as he stormed across the room. His movements were sharp and jerky, as if he couldn't control his own body anymore. The panic within him bubbled over, transforming into something dangerous, something volatile.

"Jax, wait—" I began, but it was too late.

He seized a nearby chair, gripping it white-knuckled, and slammed it into the wall with a deafening crash. The sound echoed through the room, bouncing off the cold steel walls like a gunshot. "Come on!" he screamed, his voice raw, his eyes wide with fury. "Come and get me, you son of a bitch! What are you waiting for?!"

My heart leapt into my throat. "Jax, stop!" I rushed toward him, panic rising as I watched him unravel before my eyes. His face contorted in rage, his breathing ragged and uneven. He swung the chair again, smashing it into the wall with another deafening bang, his shoulders heaving with the effort.

"Please, stop!" I begged, but he wasn't listening.

His voice grew more desperate, breath coming in gasps as he screamed at the ship, daring it to come for him. He slammed the chair down again, and this time, something shattered. It was as if the last piece of Jax snapped; he dropped the chair, his body trembling violently.

Aiden stepped forward cautiously, his voice low and

steady, trying to reach him. "Jax, you need to pull it together. We can't—"

Jax spun around, his face pale, eyes wide with terror. "You don't get it!" he shouted, his voice shaking, his entire body trembling with the force of his panic. "You don't get it, do you? This place—it's not just trying to kill us. It's inside us. It's in me. I can feel it crawling under my skin, messing with my head."

His words sent a chill through me. I stared at him, my heart pounding in my chest, desperately trying to figure out what to say, how to help. But I didn't have the answers. None of us did.

The ship was tearing us apart, feeding on our fear, twisting us into something unrecognizable. And I couldn't see a way to stop it.

Jax's hands shook uncontrollably now, his whole body vibrating with a panic that seeped into our bones—a primal fear that felt like it was eating him alive. His face was pale, eyes wide and wild, darting around the room as if trying to fend off something invisible—or perhaps something only he could see. I felt powerless, watching him unravel, knowing we were all barely holding on. Each of us was teetering on the edge of sanity, and the ship was pushing us further, daring us to fall.

Aiden stepped forward cautiously, his voice steady but laced with desperation. "We're going to get out of here, Jax," he said, his words deliberate, almost pleading. "But we need you with us. We need you to hold on."

Jax shook his head violently, breath coming in ragged gasps. His body trembled like a wire stretched too tight, ready to snap. His eyes, once filled with confidence and bravado, now blazed with terror, as if he were witnessing something the rest of us couldn't. "It's too late," he rasped, barely above a whisper. "It's already inside me."

My heart clenched painfully at his words. The Jax I knew —the one who charged ahead, cracked jokes in tough times, who seemed fearless—was slipping away, vanishing into the dark grip of the ship. And I had no idea how to bring him back.

"Jax, please," I whispered, my voice cracking. I stepped closer, reaching out as if my touch alone could tether him back to us. "We can't do this without you."

For a heartbeat, his gaze softened, a flicker of recognition sparking in his eyes. I saw the old Jax in that brief moment— the one who had always been our rock. But just as quickly, terror overtook him again. His eyes darkened, and he turned away, pacing the room like a caged animal, trapped by his own fear. He raked his fingers through his hair, pulling at the roots, his breaths quick and shallow as if he were suffocating.

I watched helplessly as the ship claimed another piece of him, wrapping its invisible tendrils around his mind. Then, out of nowhere, a cold, sharp wave of realization—or was it fear? —washed over me. Something unnatural pressed against me, suffocating, filling the room with a palpable darkness. Shadows along the walls shifted, growing larger and closer, the air thick with the stench of salt and decay.

And then, just at the edge of my hearing, I heard it.

Landon's voice.

"Sienna," the voice whispered, soft and distant, like a cold breeze brushing past my ear. "Sienna, come closer…"

I froze, my body locking up as the sound wrapped itself around me, tugging at something deep within. My heart thudded painfully in my chest as I turned toward the source of the voice, my breath catching in my throat.

In the corner of the room, just beyond the flickering light, I saw it—a shadowy figure, indistinct and hovering at the edge of darkness. My heart pounded in my ears, and the world felt like it was tilting beneath my feet.

"Landon?" I whispered, taking a hesitant step forward, my voice trembling. I didn't know what I expected—maybe him stepping forward to smile, to tell me it had all been a horrible mistake. Maybe everything would make sense again.

But when I blinked, the figure vanished. Just like that, the room was empty again, save for Jax's and Aiden's heavy breaths and the endless hum of the ship pressing down on us.

I stood frozen, my heart racing, my mind spinning as I tried to make sense of what I'd just seen—or heard. But nothing made sense anymore. Not here. Not on this ship. Nothing about this place felt real. Or maybe everything felt too real.

"Sienna, what is it?" Aiden's voice cut through the haze, pulling me back to the cold, oppressive present. His eyes were sharp, his expression tight with concern.

I shook my head, struggling to steady my breathing, trying to push the overwhelming fear back. "I... I thought I saw something," I murmured, hugging my arms to my chest as if that could hold me together.

Aiden frowned, his eyes searching my face for answers I didn't have. "What did you see?"

"I don't know," I whispered, my voice barely audible, thick with uncertainty. "But I'm starting to think Jax is right. This ship... it's in our heads."

Aiden's gaze didn't waver, but I noticed the flicker of

doubt in his eyes, the fear he struggled to suppress. He wouldn't let himself believe it—not yet.

"We'll find a way off this ship," he said, his voice low but firm. Determined. "We have to."

But deep down, uncertainty gnawed at me. The ship wasn't just haunting us; it was breaking us, piece by piece, tearing at the fragile threads that held us together until all that remained was fear, madness, and despair.

I didn't know how much longer we could endure.

CHAPTER ELEVEN

SIENNA

The cold wasn't just biting; it was invasive, creeping beneath my skin, threading through my veins, suffocating me with each breath. The air itself felt heavy, as if the ship was embedding itself deeper into my lungs with every inhale. The corridors twisted in on themselves, a never-ending labyrinth intent on disorienting us, trapping us within its steel belly.

Aiden's hand wrapped firmly around mine—a lifeline in the chaos. His palm was warm and solid, yet I could feel the faint tremor in his fingers, an unsettling admission that he, too, was not immune to the ship's rising terror. He had always been our anchor, the steady one who kept us from unraveling when everything went sideways. But now, I sensed the cracks forming in him, and that terrified me more than the ship itself.

We had been walking for what felt like hours, each step a futile effort. There was no end in sight—no escape, no promise of daylight or freedom. Each turn seemed to lead us deeper into the ship's heart, where the walls constricted, drawing closer as if the ship were intentionally shifting, manipulating our path, ensnaring us in its twisted embrace.

"We're close, Sienna," Aiden said, his voice low and measured, though I could hear the strain beneath it. He was trying to convince me—perhaps even himself. His usual confidence frayed at the edges, unraveling in the oppressive silence that surrounded us.

I glanced up at him, my heart heavy with the weight of our situation. His face, usually strong and resolute, now appeared pale and gaunt, eyes shadowed by exhaustion and fear. Those familiar eyes—once my anchor—now looked haunted, clouded with doubt and uncertainty. "Do you really believe that?" I whispered, my voice barely audible, as if fearing the answer he might give.

He hesitated for just a heartbeat before nodding, his expression a mixture of determination and desperation. "We have to believe it," he said, squeezing my hand a little tighter. "We're getting off this ship. I promise."

I longed to believe him. I needed to. Yet the ship's suffocating presence weighed heavier with every passing second. The darkness surrounding us wasn't merely physical—it seeped into my mind, clouding my thoughts, crushing my hope. Still, Aiden was my light, the only tether to reality amidst the chaos. Even if his light flickered, even if we dangled by a thread, I clung to it.

We paused for a moment in a small alcove, the cold metal walls pressing against my back as I leaned into him. His arms wrapped around me, pulling me close, and I buried my face in his chest, inhaling his familiar scent—salt, sweat, and something unmistakably Aiden. For a brief moment, the chaos outside faded, and it was just the two of us. The ship's haunting presence receded, if only for a heartbeat.

"We'll get out of here," he whispered, his lips brushing against my forehead as he kissed me softly. "I won't let anything happen to you."

I pulled back slightly, my eyes searching his face, seeking his reassurance. "What if we can't? What if there's no way off this ship?" My voice wavered, betraying the fear I had fought so hard to suppress.

His gaze softened as he tucked a loose strand of hair behind my ear. "We'll find a way," he said quietly, his voice imbued with a gentle certainty that I desperately wanted to believe. Then he leaned down and kissed me tenderly. His lips were warm, a stark contrast to the freezing air around us, and for that brief moment, the ship and its horrors faded away. There was no danger, no looming death—just us, holding on to each other in the only way we knew how.

When we finally pulled apart, Aiden rested his forehead against mine, his breath warm and steady against my skin. "You keep me going," he whispered, his voice barely audible yet filled with emotion. "You always have."

Tears stung my eyes, but I forced a smile, blinking them back. "And you keep me sane," I murmured, gripping his hand as if it were the only thing preventing me from falling apart completely.

But reality crashed down all too quickly. The ship wasn't done with us. We hadn't found the deck yet, and it felt like every hallway we ventured down led us deeper into the ship's twisted core. Every turn brought us back to where we started, the layout shifting as if it were alive. It was toying with us, trapping us in its endless maze.

Finally, Aiden made a decision, his voice steady despite the chaos swirling around us. "If we can't find the lifeboats, maybe we can restart the engine and sail ourselves out of this nightmare." His words were firm and decisive, and I clung to them because I needed something—anything—that resembled a plan. Aiden always had a plan; he always knew what to do when everything else fell apart. But this time, something felt different. A sense of unease gnawed at the edges of my mind, a faint whisper of dread warning me that we were venturing into territory far darker than anything we had faced before.

We had been searching for a map—anything that could guide us to the lifeboats—but every wall we passed was barren. The last map Aiden had found was fixed to a bulkhead, a small hope in the vast sea of confusion, but now there was nothing. The ship had swallowed up every trace of direction and every scrap of logic, leaving us to navigate its twisting, shifting halls alone.

I could feel the ship's malevolence growing stronger with each step we took. It wasn't just in the cold air or the suffocating darkness pressing in from all sides; it was in the way the walls seemed to breathe, in the way the floor creaked and groaned as if it were alive, shifting beneath our feet. The deeper we went, the more it felt like the ship was tightening its grip on us, pulling us into its cold, empty heart. And yet, Aiden pressed on.

We followed because we had to. I had no choice. I trusted Aiden, but a knot of fear twisted in my stomach, refusing to loosen no matter how tightly I clung to the warmth of his hand.

As we turned another corner, the dim lights overhead flickering weakly, we saw it—a rusted metal sign bolted to the wall, its letters barely legible beneath layers of grime and rust.

Engine Room. The arrow pointed down a narrow staircase, the dark void below beckoning us deeper. My stomach clenched, the knot of fear tightening further.

"We're close," Aiden murmured, his hand gripping mine a little tighter as he read the sign. His eyes flicked down the staircase, his expression unreadable. But I saw it—just for a moment—the flicker of doubt, the shadow of fear in his gaze. He wasn't sure either.

I swallowed hard, my throat dry. "Aiden, are you sure this is the right call?"

He turned to me, his face pale but determined. "We don't have many options left, Sienna. If we can get the engines running, we might be able to steer this ship out of here." His voice was steady, but I could hear the strain, the cracks forming beneath the surface. He was holding it together for all of us, but even Aiden had his limits.

I nodded, not trusting myself to speak. The words I wanted to say—What if we're making it worse? What if the ship doesn't let us go?—remained lodged in my throat. I couldn't voice them, not now. Not when we were this far in.

We descended the stairs, each step echoing hollowly in the cold, metallic space. The air down here was even thicker, almost choking, and the temperature dropped with every step. It was as though the ship knew where we were going, as though it wanted us down here in the bowels of its dark, twisted body.

Finally, we reached the bottom of the stairs, and the narrow hallway stretched out before us. It was darker down here, the lights overhead flickering weakly, casting long shadows that danced along the walls. The sound of machinery hummed faintly in the distance, but it wasn't comforting—it was ominous, like the ship was waking up, its malevolent presence growing stronger the closer we got.

Aiden squeezed my hand once more before letting go, his eyes scanning the hallway ahead. "Stay close," he said, his voice low, barely more than a whisper. "We're almost there."

I nodded, my heart pounding in my chest as we moved forward, each step taking us deeper into the ship's cold, empty heart. I could feel it now, more than ever—that pull, that dark presence wrapping around me, whispering in my ear, You're not leaving. You'll never leave.

But I pushed it down, forcing myself to keep moving. Because Aiden and Jax were here. If I had any chance of getting out of this nightmare, it was with them.

We had to survive.

CHAPTER TWELVE

AIDEN

The engine room was larger than I had imagined—a cavernous, decaying space filled with rusting machinery and looming metal parts that looked untouched for decades. The heavy stench of oil and damp rot hung in the air, clinging to everything. Each breath felt thick, as if suffocating me from the inside out, but I couldn't afford to let fear take over. Not now. Not in front of Sienna.

I glanced back at Jax, who had been walking silently behind us the whole time, his usually loud and brash demeanor reduced to a tense, quiet presence. His face was drawn tight, his eyes hollow, as if he were barely holding himself together. The madness that had overtaken him earlier still simmered just beneath the surface, but for now, he was calm. Too calm. It made me uneasy.

"This is it," I said, forcing my voice to remain steady as I approached the rusted control panel. My fingers ran over the cold, corroded metal, searching for anything that could bring this place back to life. "If we can get this thing started, maybe we can steer the ship out of here."

Sienna stood beside me, her arms wrapped around herself as if trying to ward off the cold that had seeped into every corner of the ship. Her face was pale, her wide eyes filled with apprehension. She looked fragile, her strength wavering under the oppressive weight of the ship's malevolence.

"Are you sure this will work?" she asked, her voice barely above a whisper. Fear lingered there, but so did a glimmer of hope—a hope I wasn't sure I could give her.

I nodded, even though the truth was, I wasn't sure of anything anymore. The ship had warped everything, twisting reality around us until it was impossible to discern what was real. But I had to try. "I'll figure it out. Stay close, okay?"

She nodded, her teeth worrying at her bottom lip as she watched me work, the tension radiating off her in waves. I could feel her fear, her doubt, clawing at me because I hated putting her through this. I hated that we were all trapped in this hell. But I had to believe we could still find a way out. I had to keep her safe.

Behind us, Jax hovered near the door, his eyes darting around the room, fingers twitching at his sides. He was jittery, restless, barely holding it together. The ship had already taken so much from him—had taken Landon and twisted his mind. I could feel it gnawing at him, breaking him down piece by piece. I didn't know how much longer he could hold on.

I pulled a lever, the rusted metal groaning as it gave way beneath my hands. The machinery roared to life, a deafening sound reverberating through the room, metal grinding against metal in a horrible, screeching symphony. It was working—the engine was awakening. Gears turned, and the room shuddered with the force of it. For a brief moment, hope flickered within me, burning bright and desperate.

But then, without warning, the machinery lurched. Not just the gears—everything in the room seemed to come alive. Massive metal arms and parts shifted wildly, spinning out of control with a speed and violence that defied logic.

I tried to back away, to escape the chaos, but I couldn't. An invisible force gripped me—like hands clamping down on my shoulders, holding me in place. Panic surged through me, but I was frozen, unable to move. Dread settled in, cold and absolute, tightening around my chest.

"Sienna!" I shouted, but my voice was swallowed by the roar of the engine, the metallic grinding so loud it felt like it was rattling my bones. I saw her turn, her face pale with terror, but before she could reach me, the machinery lurched again.

A massive steel arm swung across the room, moving faster than anything that size should have been able to. I barely registered what was happening before it slammed into me, crushing me against the cold, unforgiving wall.

Pain exploded through my chest—white-hot and searing—stealing the breath from my lungs. My vision blurred, the deafening roar of the engine drowning out everything else, my heartbeat pounding loud and frantic in my ears. I could hear Sienna scream, a raw, desperate sound that felt distant, as if it were echoing from somewhere far away.

I struggled to move, to pull myself free, but the force holding me down was too strong. I was pinned, helpless, the weight of the metal crushing the life from me.

"Sienna..." I tried to call out, but the word barely escaped my lips. My vision faded further, the edges growing dark. I could feel my life slipping away, draining like water through my fingers.

I wanted to tell her I loved her. I wanted to urge her to run, to escape, to survive. But the words wouldn't come.

And then… everything went black.

CHAPTER THIRTEEN

SIENNA

I t all happened so fast—too fast for me to comprehend. One moment, Aiden was at the controls, focused and determined; the next, he was slammed against the wall, crushed by the engine's massive, shifting parts. The grinding metal swallowed my scream, and for a split second, the world stopped. Everything blurred into chaos.

"Aiden!" My voice cracked as I stumbled toward him, my legs barely holding me up. Each breath came shallow and ragged, as if the ship itself was siphoning the air from my lungs. He lay crumpled, his body twisted in a way that made me want to look away, but I couldn't. I couldn't.

I collapsed to my knees in front of him, my hands shaking uncontrollably as I reached for him. "No, no, no," I whispered, my voice breaking, my heart pounding in my chest like it was trying to escape. His skin was still warm, but blood dripped from his lips—a slow, terrible trickle that sent icy dread coursing through me.

"Aiden, please, no…" I choked, tears streaming down my face uncontrollably. My voice came out broken and frantic as I cradled his face in my trembling hands. "Please, don't do this. Don't leave me. Please, Aiden, please—" My words turned into sobs, my heart tearing apart as his eyes fluttered closed, his breath faltering.

And then… nothing. His body lay still, the last vestiges of life slipping away, leaving behind only cold, lifeless flesh. Aiden—my anchor, the one who always knew what to do, the one who kept me grounded—was gone.

I was frozen, my hands still cradling his face, unwilling to let go, unable to accept that he was truly gone. The emptiness swelled inside me, threatening to drown me whole. A scream tore from my throat, but it didn't sound like my voice. It was someone else's—someone shattered beyond repair.

Behind me, a wild, ragged noise broke through the chaos— Jax. He paced frantically, his hands tugging at his hair, his eyes glassy and frantic with panic. "This isn't real. This can't be real!" He slammed his fist against the wall, again and again, until his knuckles bled. "We're all going to die! This ship is killing us! It's going to take us all!"

He was spiraling, unraveling right before my eyes, but I couldn't stop him. I felt helpless—Aiden was dead, and something inside me had died with him.

"Jax, stop…" I tried to plead, but my voice came out hoarse, barely audible through my sobs. He didn't hear me. Instead, he ranted, screaming at the ship, cursing it, daring it to come for him next. His fear had morphed into pure madness, and I could see he was lost, just like Aiden.

"You're next! You hear me?" Jax shouted, his voice cracked and raw. "Come on! Take me! You've already taken everything else!" In a fit of rage, he grabbed a wrench from the floor and hurled it across the room, the metal clanging loudly as it collided with the wall. His entire body shook with fury, his breath coming in erratic gasps.

But I couldn't focus on anything but the cold weight of Aiden in my arms. My world had collapsed, and nothing made sense anymore. The ship wasn't just killing us; it was breaking us, piece by piece, until there was nothing left. I could feel it pulling me down, sinking its claws into my mind, blurring everything into an endless nightmare.

Aiden was gone. Landon was gone. And now Jax... Jax was slipping away from me, disappearing into the madness, just like everything else.

I was going to end up alone. Completely and utterly alone.

I pressed my forehead against Aiden's, the sobs wracking my body as I whispered, "I can't do this without you. I can't... I can't..." My voice trailed off, swallowed by the hum of the ship, drowned out by the hollow sound of my heart shattering in my chest.

The ship had won. I didn't know if I could survive what it had taken from me.

CHAPTER FOURTEEN

SIENNA

Aiden was gone. Landon was gone. And now Jax—my last thread of sanity—was unraveling faster than I could reach him.

"Jax, please," I whispered, my voice barely breaking through the thick air of the dimly lit engine room. The weight of Aiden's death was still fresh, like an open wound that wouldn't stop bleeding. My body was numb from the grief, from the fear, and from the growing certainty that we were trapped in this nightmare for good. But seeing Jax like this—cracking, losing himself—ripped at me in a way I couldn't fully comprehend. I wanted to grab hold of him, to pull him back before he slipped into the same darkness that had taken everything else from us. But his eyes—wide, unfocused—darted around the room like a wild animal, trapped and desperate.

"We're doomed!" he shouted, his voice cracking under the weight of his panic. He kicked at the nearest piece of machinery, the metal groaning under the force of his anger. The sharp clang of metal on metal echoed violently through the room, the sound drilling into my skull, setting my nerves on edge. "Don't you see it, Sienna? We're trapped! This ship—it's playing with us. It's laughing at us!"

"Jax, stop!" I begged, my voice trembling as I took a cautious step toward him. My heart was pounding, each beat a painful thud in my chest. But he didn't stop. He didn't even hear me—or maybe he didn't want to hear me. He was too far gone now, lost in the suffocating grip of his own fear.

His hands balled into fists at his sides, breathing coming in short, ragged bursts. When he turned to face me, his expression twisted with rage, his eyes burned with an intensity that terrified me. "Landon's dead! Aiden's dead! We're all going to die here, just like them. This place... it wants us, Sienna! Don't you get it? It's going to take us one by one, and there's nothing we can do!"

I flinched, his words hitting me like a physical blow. My chest tightened, thoughts spiraling, but I couldn't allow myself to fall into the same abyss that had swallowed Jax. I had to believe there was still a way out, even if it eluded me.

"Jax, please," I pleaded, stepping closer, my hands outstretched as if I could physically pull him back from the edge. "We can still get out of here. We just need to think. We need to stick together."

But before I could finish, his desperation reached a fever pitch. He bolted, a sudden, frantic surge of energy that sent my stomach plummeting. He raced out of the engine room, his footsteps echoing wildly down the corridor, like a man fleeing from something only he could see.

"Jax! Wait!" I shouted, my voice laced with rising panic as I stumbled after him. My legs felt weak, barely holding me up, the cold grip of fear tightening around me. I chased after him, my breath ragged, heart hammering in my chest as he disappeared around the corner, his figure swallowed by the ship's labyrinth of twisting, shadowed hallways.

I didn't know where Jax was heading, but I couldn't lose him—not after everything we'd been through. I couldn't let this ship take him, too.

"Jax!" I screamed again, pushing myself harder, but the ship's darkness seemed to close in around me, swallowing my voice, pulling me deeper into its nightmare.

I fought to keep up, my legs burning, my heart racing as we tore through the twisting hallways. The oppressive energy of the ship tightened around us, the walls narrowing, the flickering lights overhead casting everything in an eerie, unnatural glow.

Then, Jax's scream sliced through the heavy silence, his voice raw and shredded by terror. "Come on!" he bellowed into the void, challenging the ship as if it were a living beast, something sentient watching us. "Come get me, you bastard! What are you waiting for?!"

Dread settled deeper into my bones, cold and unforgiving. He wasn't just losing it—he was throwing himself at the mercy of the ship, begging it to finish what it had started with Aiden and Landon. My heart twisted painfully in my chest, a chaotic mess of grief, fear, and desperation as I sprinted after him, unwilling to let the last piece of my world crumble.

We burst into the dining room—the very place where we first sensed that something was horribly wrong. The expansive room unfolded before us, its massive chandeliers hanging like jewels of doom above, their crystal prisms refracting dim light and casting eerie shadows across the polished floor. The shadows danced, flickering like silent ghosts, shifting with the ship's gentle sway. It felt haunted, hollow.

At the far end of the room, a giant glass window framed the black, churning ocean, stretching endlessly in all directions, as if the world had vanished, leaving only water and darkness. The vastness of it made my head spin, a dizzying reminder of how utterly alone we were—adrift in nothingness.

Jax stood in front of the window, his chest heaving, palms pressed hard against the cold glass. His reflection was a ghost of the man he used to be—wild hair, hollow eyes, and the unmistakable look of someone broken beyond repair. He stared at his own reflection as if seeing a stranger.

"Look at it," he whispered, his voice hoarse and barely audible above the creaking of the ship. "Just… look at it." His gaze fixed on the endless sea. "We're in the middle of nowhere. There's no one coming for us. No one to save us. We're… we're already dead."

The agony in his voice shattered the fragile thread of hope I had been clinging to. I slowed my approach, my heart breaking for him—for us. Jax, the one who had always been so vibrant, so invincible, was unraveling right before me. The same man who had kept us laughing, who had propelled us forward, now stood on the brink of complete despair.

"We're not dead, Jax," I said softly, though my voice trembled, weak against the rising tide of hopelessness. "We're still here. We're still fighting."

He shook his head violently, his fingers curling into fists as he slammed them against the window. The sound echoed like a gunshot through the vast, empty room. "No, we're not!" His voice cracked, raw with frustration. "This ship… it's feeding off us, Sienna. It's using us, playing with us like we're nothing but toys. It's waiting for the right moment, and when it's done with us, we'll be just like the others—like all those photos on the walls."

My stomach knotted at his words. I stepped closer, my hand trembling as I gently placed it on his shoulder, feeling the tension in his body, the fear vibrating beneath his skin. I needed to pull him back from the brink, from the madness clawing at his mind. "Jax, you're not thinking clearly. We can figure this out. We just need to—"

He whirled around to face me, and for a moment, I hardly recognized him. His eyes were wild, blazing with anger and desperation—a storm of emotion threatening to swallow him whole. "There's nothing to figure out, Sienna!" he shouted, his words reverberating through the cavernous room, bouncing off the walls as if mocking us. "It's over! We're done! Don't you get it? We're never getting out of here!"

I flinched at the venom in his voice, but I didn't back down. I couldn't. He was all I had left, the last tether keeping me from floating off into the same dark place that had claimed the others. "Jax, please…" My voice wavered as I stepped closer. "We've already lost so much. Don't let this ship take you too."

For a moment—a fleeting second—I saw something shift in his eyes—recognition, perhaps, or the flicker of the Jax I knew. But it vanished as quickly as it had come, swallowed by the crushing weight of the fear dragging him under. He backed away from me, his chest rising and falling with ragged breaths, fists still clenched at his sides.

Before I could say anything else, the ship groaned again— louder this time, more insistent, as if responding to Jax's challenge. The sound reverberated through the room, and suddenly, the chandeliers overhead began to sway, their crystals clinking together like wind chimes in a storm.

"Jax, get back!" I shouted, panic rising in my chest as I glanced up at the massive glass fixtures swinging precariously above us.

But Jax didn't move. He stood frozen, his gaze fixed on the window, as if he couldn't tear himself away from the dark expanse of the sea. And then, with a deafening crack, the chandelier above him came crashing down.

"No!" The word tore from my throat, but it was already too late.

The chandelier shattered with a violent crash, the explosion of glass and metal filling the room with a sharp, terrible sound. Jagged shards glistened like deadly rain as they scattered across the floor, but all I could focus on was Jax. He lay beneath the wreckage, crushed by the twisted metal and shattered glass.

My body moved on instinct, legs buckling as I dropped to my knees beside him. My hands shook as I frantically tried to pull the debris off him, fingers slipping against the cold, slick metal and blood.

"Jax!" I choked out, my voice raw and desperate. His eyes were open, staring blankly at the ceiling, void of the life that had once burned so brightly within him. Gone. Just like that.

The blood pooling around him spread quickly, staining the floor and soaking into my clothes as I knelt beside him, my sobs shaking my entire body. His hand—once so warm and full of energy—was cold and limp in mine. No pulse. No breath.

"Jax, please," I whimpered, tears falling onto his chest. "You can't leave me. Not like this. Please."

But there was nothing left. No response. The vibrant, fearless Jax who had laughed through every storm, who had stood by my side through every nightmare, was gone. And I was alone. Completely, utterly alone.

I collapsed beside him, fingers clutching his lifeless hand as if holding on could somehow pull him back from the edge. But it was no use. The ship had taken him, just like it had taken Landon, just like it had taken Aiden. It had devoured them all, and now… now it had its sights set on me.

The cold reality settled in my chest, a weight too heavy to bear. There was no one left. No one to fight for, no one to hold on to. Just me and this damned, haunted ship, its malevolent presence wrapping tighter around me with every breath I took.

I stared at the broken remains of the chandelier—the twisted metal and splintered glass that had stolen the last piece of my world. The room felt hollow, too quiet; the oppressive silence broken only by the faint echo of my ragged breaths. Jax's body lay beneath me like the final, cruel punctuation on the horror we'd endured.

I pressed my forehead against his chest, straining to hear a heartbeat that would never come, clinging to the hope that perhaps, just perhaps, I was wrong. But deep down, I knew the truth. I had recognized it from the moment the ship claimed its first victim.

This place—it had never intended to let us go. It had been toying with us, breaking us, feeding off our fear and despair until there was nothing left to give.

And now, it was coming for me.

The weight of that realization settled heavily in my gut, a cold, gnawing dread that sent a shiver down my spine. There was no one left to help me. No one to cling to for hope or comfort. The ship had stripped me of everything I held dear.

I lifted my head, staring at Jax's pale, lifeless face. His features were frozen in shock, as if he couldn't quite believe this was how it ended. Neither could I. He had been so full of life, so invincible. And now he was nothing more than another victim of this cursed ship.

I wiped my tears with the back of my hand, the salty sting mingling with the metallic taste of blood that lingered in the air. My grief was a storm inside me, but beneath it, something darker stirred—a quiet, simmering rage. The ship had taken everything from me. And now it sought the last of my spirit, my very will to survive.

CHAPTER FIFTEEN

SIENNA

The silence was crushing, thick and oppressive, as if the very air around me conspired with the ship to smother me. It pressed down from every direction, not just from the outside but from within, burrowing deep into my chest. It was the cold I felt in my bones, the air that gnawed at my skin—an unsettling presence embedded in every corner of the ship, lurking just beyond my sight in the spaces where shadows writhed and shifted like living things.

I forced myself to my feet, though my legs trembled beneath me, weak and unsteady as if they might give out at any moment. I couldn't stay down. I couldn't afford to collapse, not with Jax's blood spreading in dark, sticky pools across the floor, seeping into the ship as if it belonged there. My throat tightened, a sob clawing its way up, but I swallowed it, forcing the tears back. There was no room left for grief. Not anymore.

The ship wanted me. I felt it now, more than ever, pulsing in the very walls around me like a heartbeat—slow and deliberate, as if savoring my fear. The air hummed with it, alive with something dark and ancient. It whispered my name—Sienna—

a cruel, haunting reminder that I was the only one left. The ship had claimed Landon, taken Aiden, and now it had Jax. One by one, it fed on their despair until there was no one left but me.

And it wanted me to break.

I stumbled forward, unable to look back at Jax's lifeless body, his face forever etched in my memory. They were all gone now—every last one of them. My heart pounded in my chest, each beat hard and erratic, the panic rising like a flood, but I couldn't let it consume me. Not yet.

The hallway stretched out before me, long and endless, the lights flickering weakly overhead, casting everything in a dull, sickly glow. Every shadow I passed seemed to shift, to move with purpose, creeping toward me as if it were alive, waiting to swallow me whole. I hugged myself tightly, trying to stave off the trembling that had taken hold of me. My footsteps echoed in the emptiness, the sound hollow and haunting—a reminder of how alone I truly was.

As I wandered aimlessly through the ship's maze of rusted metal and decay, the memories flooded back. Their voices echoed in my mind—Landon's laughter, Aiden's calm words, Jax's defiant shouting. Each memory twisted like a knife, digging deeper into the wounds I thought would never heal.

"Sienna…"

The voice was soft, barely more than a whisper, yet it sliced through the silence like a blade. My heart skipped a beat, my breath catching in my throat. I knew that voice. I'd know it anywhere. It was Landon's, his familiar, soothing tone that had once anchored me and made me feel safe. Now, it sent a chill crawling up my spine.

I froze, my body stiffening as I turned slowly, my eyes

scanning the empty hallway. There was nothing—only shadows and the endless cold. But the voice continued, closer now, more insistent.

"Sienna... come back..."

My pulse raced as I stood rooted to the spot, unable to move. I wanted to believe it, wanted to believe that somehow Landon was still with me, still out there, waiting. But I knew better. I had watched him die. I had held him as life drained from his body.

And yet, the voice persisted, pulling at me and calling me deeper into the ship's clutches. "Come back to me, Sienna. We're waiting..."

My hands balled into fists at my sides, nails digging into my palms as I struggled to resist the pull, but my feet began to move of their own accord. It wasn't just Landon's voice I heard now—it was Aiden's and Jax's, their whispers swirling around me like a ghostly wind, beckoning me forward.

My breath hitched, panic tightening its grip on my chest as I stumbled forward, the shadows pressing closer with each step. I was losing myself, slipping further into the ship's dark embrace. Deep down, I started to wonder if I even had the strength to fight it.

My heart clenched painfully, every beat a reminder of the unbearable grief pressing down on me. "Landon?" My voice cracked, fragile and broken, barely escaping my lips as I stumbled forward, hands reaching for something—someone—that wasn't there. "Landon, where are you?"

The only response was the soft, eerie hum of the ship, the metallic groans echoing through its hollow corridors. Yet, the voice lingered, teasing me and drawing me deeper into the darkness. It tugged at the edges of my mind, a faint pull that refused to let go.

I kept walking, my steps slow and unsteady, as if the ship itself guided me toward something unseen, something it had long been waiting to reveal. The shadows around me stretched and shifted, twisting into shapes that felt achingly familiar. For a fleeting moment, I thought I saw them—Landon, standing just out of reach, his figure hazy and shimmering like a mirage. Beside him, Aiden stood, his hand outstretched, waiting for me, his face filled with the same warmth that once made me feel safe. Behind them, Jax's crooked smile flickered in the dim light, a reminder of the life we had before everything went wrong.

"Don't leave me..." I whispered, the plea tearing at my throat as my fingers reached out toward them. But the moment I stepped closer, they vanished, dissolving back into the shadows and leaving nothing but the emptiness that had haunted me since their deaths.

Panic surged, tightening around my chest like a vise. The cold, thick air grew denser, suffocating me with each shallow breath. The walls seemed to press inward, closing the distance between me and the endless dark. Then, I heard it—the ship. It whispered to me, its voice low and insidious, wrapping itself around my mind.

"There's no escape, Sienna." The words slithered through the air, creeping into my thoughts like poison. "You're the last. The final piece."

I stumbled backward, shaking my head violently, as if I could dislodge the truth it was forcing upon me. My hands flew to my ears, desperate to block out the sound, to drown out the venomous voice consuming my every thought. "No," I whispered, trembling. "No, I won't let you have me."

But the ship was relentless. The shadows twisted once more, taking on shapes I could never forget. Aiden's face emerged from the dark, his eyes wide and pleading, filled with a desperation that shattered me all over again. "Sienna, please. Don't leave me…"

I could barely breathe, the words lodged in my throat like shards of glass. "I can't," I sobbed, collapsing against the cold metal wall, my body shaking under the weight of it all. "I'm trying, but I can't save you."

His face flickered like a dying flame, and then Jax was there, his voice raw with pain, his expression steeped in desperation. "We're waiting, Sienna. We're all waiting for you…"

My heart raced, the rhythm erratic, each beat feeling like a punch to my chest. I could feel the pull of their voices, tugging at the shattered pieces of my soul, begging me to believe they were still with me. But deep down, beneath the crushing weight of grief and exhaustion, I knew the truth: they were gone. The ship had consumed them, twisted them into something unrecognizable, and now it was coming for me.

I pressed my back against the cold metal, sliding down until I was curled into myself on the floor, my knees pulled tightly to my chest. The ship's whispers grew louder, more insistent, filling the space around me and drowning out everything else. It seeped into my mind, warping my thoughts and distorting my reality until I could no longer discern what was real.

It's over, I thought, the words sinking into me like stones

dragging me to the bottom of a dark, endless ocean. There's no way out.

I closed my eyes, allowing the oppressive darkness to wash over me. In that moment, the horrifying truth became clear: the ship had been feeding off us from the beginning. It had lured us in, letting us believe we could fight, could escape, but it had never intended to let us go. We were its prisoners, its prey, and now, with the others gone, I was the last one left.

You're mine now, the ship seemed to whisper, its voice wrapping around me like a shroud, cold and final.

I was alone—completely and utterly alone in the dark, with no one left to save me.

CHAPTER SIXTEEN

SIENNA

I was alone. But not really.

Their voices lingered—Landon, Aiden, Jax—always just beyond the edge of hearing. Soft whispers tugged at the corners of my mind, drawing me deeper into the ship's labyrinth. I couldn't tell how long I had been walking; time had lost all meaning, its passage a distant memory from a life I could barely recognize anymore. This place—this ship—it had stolen everything from me. Every corridor I turned into was a mirror of the last, each hallway an endless stretch of decaying steel and rust. The air was stale, thick with the scent of salt mingling with something darker, something rotten. It clung to my skin, heavy and cold, as if the ship itself was trying to pull me into its depths.

"Landon?" My voice barely broke the silence, a fragile thread that cracked as soon as it left my lips. My heart twisted painfully in my chest as his name hung in the air, unanswered. His laughter echoed in my mind—sharp and warm, the kind of sound that filled a room and made the world feel bright again. I remembered how his eyes would light up when he talked about our future, the dreams we had woven together, the places we were meant to explore. That future, once so vivid and tangible, had vanished like smoke, leaving only the shadows of what could have been.

"Do you remember the wedding you dreamed of?" I asked, my voice shaking, barely holding itself together. "The one we never had?"

Silence. No answer. But there, just beyond the flickering shadows, I thought I glimpsed him. His tall, familiar frame leaned casually against the wall, just as he always did, a playful, lopsided grin tugging at his lips. My heart clenched painfully, the edges of reality blurring as I let myself believe— if only for a moment—that he was real. That he was standing there, waiting for me.

"I always said we didn't need a wedding, didn't I?" I continued, my voice trembling under the weight of grief. "That it was just a piece of paper, a formality. But I lied, Landon. I wanted it too. I wanted the dress, the vows, the way you would've looked at me as if I were the only person in the world."

I blinked, and he was gone. A trick of the light, a cruel illusion conjured by the ship. My throat tightened as the emptiness gnawed at my insides, hollowing me out until all that remained was the unbearable weight of loss. The ship had taken them all —Landon, Aiden, Jax—swallowed them whole, piece by piece, until nothing remained but their ghosts. Their faces, their voices, all just memories now, twisted and distorted by the ship's malevolence.

I kept walking; what else was there to do? The hollow echo of my footsteps filled the silence—a lonely sound that bounced off the metal walls. The floor beneath my boots felt unsteady, as if the ship were shifting beneath me, pulling me further into its depths, into its endless, dark heart. I had no idea where I was going, no sense of direction, no plan. Every step felt heavier than the last, as if the ship were dragging me down, as if it were winning. And maybe it was. Maybe it already had.

My breath hitched as I passed another shadowy corridor, my pulse quickening with a flash of recognition that I knew wasn't real, but I couldn't stop myself from hoping.

"Aiden?"

His name slipped from my lips before I could stop it, his memory crashing over me like a tidal wave. His wild laugh and that smile he wore like armor filled my chest with a pain so sharp it almost brought me to my knees. Jax had always been larger than life, the kind of person who dared the world to knock him down—and somehow, it never did. Until now.

In my mind, I could see him standing at the far end of the corridor, arms casually crossed, his smirk tugging at the corners of his lips, as if none of this could ever touch him. As if even this cursed ship couldn't break him.

"Remember Egypt?" I whispered, my voice trembling as it cut through the suffocating silence. "You always said we'd go. Sail down the Nile. Climb the pyramids, even if we weren't supposed to." My throat constricted, an ache tightening there. "God, Aiden, I wish we had."

Instinctively, I reached out, my hand stretching toward the shadowy figure where Aiden once stood. But as my fingers grazed the air, he vanished—fading into nothing, swallowed by the ship's endless darkness, just like the others. My breath hitched, a sob rising in my chest, nearly strangling me before I swallowed it down. I didn't want to cry. I didn't want to give the ship the satisfaction of knowing it was breaking me.

But it was. The ship was winning. I could feel it creeping into my mind, twisting everything I thought I knew, distorting memories, blurring the line between reality and illusion. I wasn't sure if I had ever been sane or if this ship had warped me from the moment I stepped on board. Just like Aiden. Just like Landon. Soon, there would be nothing left of me but shattered fragments of who I used to be.

I forced my feet to keep moving. One step, then another. But it didn't matter. The hallway stretched endlessly before me —no doors, no windows, no hint of escape. Just the oppressive dark, suffocating, pressing in from all sides. The air was thick with the stench of salt and decay, as if the ship were rotting from the inside out. Each breath felt like a struggle, the weight of it crushing my chest, squeezing the life from my lungs.

"Why didn't I give you that baby, Jax?" I whispered into the void, my voice cracking under the weight of regret. "You wanted it so badly, and I kept saying no. I said it wasn't the right time, that we weren't ready." My breath hitched, a sob clawing its way up my throat. "But the truth is... I was scared. Scared of losing all of you, scared of everything. And now... I've lost you all anyway."

Then the tears came, hot and relentless, streaming down my face as I staggered through the ship's haunted corridors. I felt like I was walking blindly—no direction, no purpose—just moving because stopping meant surrender. But I was losing my mind. The ship was digging deeper into me, picking apart my thoughts, unraveling every last piece of myself until there'd be nothing left but echoes. I would be just another ghost, wandering these twisted halls, trapped forever.

But something inside me still clung to hope. Faint, flickering—but there. I wasn't ready to give in. Not yet.

I needed to find the deck. I needed to see the sky, feel the wind on my face one last time. Maybe I couldn't outrun the ship, maybe I couldn't save the others, but I could still save myself from the same fate. If I could just reach the edge, gaze at the ocean below, I could escape on my own terms. I could jump—choose my own way out, rather than let the ship claim me like it had claimed them.

I took a deep breath, my heart pounding as I steeled myself. I wasn't giving up. Not yet.

But every turn led to another hallway, every step dragging me deeper into the ship's twisted, pulsating heart. The walls closed in, warping, shifting—as if the ship itself was alive, toying with me. There was no map, no exit, no sign of the world outside this cursed vessel. The ship was a labyrinth, breathing around me, its cold metal veins pulsing with malevolence. I was trapped, swallowed whole by its unrelenting darkness.

You're mine now, the ship whispered, its voice slithering through the corridors, wrapping around me like a suffocating mist. It wasn't a sound—not exactly. It was a presence, a sinister force pressing into my mind, tightening its grip with every step. You can't escape me.

A shiver shot down my spine, and for a moment, I faltered, the weight of its words crushing me. The ship was inside me now, crawling beneath my skin, rooting itself in my bones. I could feel its hunger, the way it fed off my fear, grief, and exhaustion. But I couldn't let it break me—not yet.

"I won't," I whispered, more to myself than to the ship. "I won't let you win."

But the words felt hollow, even to me. I was losing. The ship was tightening its hold, the walls pulsing in rhythm with my racing heart. Every corner I turned was the same one I'd just passed. Every step grew heavier, slower, like I was sinking into quicksand, with no way out.

They're gone, the ship hissed, its voice a low growl that made my skin crawl. Landon, Aiden, Jax—they're mine now. You'll be joining them soon.

I ignored it; I had to. If I let it in—if I let that voice burrow into my soul—it would be over. The ship would consume me, just as it had consumed them. I had to believe—needed to believe—there was still a way out. That I could still break free, even if I were lost in the darkest corners of this monstrous place.

"Landon, Aiden, Jax," I whispered, their names catching in my throat—a broken prayer that tasted like ash on my lips. "I'm so sorry. I'm sorry I couldn't save you; I tried. I tried so hard."

My voice cracked, grief overwhelming me, but I pushed it down, burying it deep inside. There was no time for mourning —no time to crumble beneath the weight of all I'd lost. Not if I wanted to survive.

"I won't let it take me, too," I muttered, the words barely audible—more of a plea than a declaration. But even as I spoke, I felt the last threads of hope slipping through my fingers, unraveling into the ship's infinite darkness.

The whispers grew louder, pressing in on all sides—a chorus of voices I recognized and didn't all at once. They echoed through the corridors, weaving through the air like the wind before a storm. I swore I heard Jax's laugh, Landon's voice calling my name, Aiden's steady reassurances—faint and distant, like they were trapped just out of reach. But I knew better. The ship was playing with me—feeding on my desperation, warping reality until I couldn't tell what was real anymore.

And then the truth settled into me like a weight too heavy to carry. There was no escape. I was alone in the dark. And it was only a matter of time before the ship claimed me, too.

CHAPTER SEVENTEEN

SIENNA

The whispers had become unbearable—a constant chorus of voices swirling in the corners of my mind, growing louder and more relentless with every passing second.

They weren't merely words; they were memories—jagged and broken fragments of the people I had loved and lost.

Landon's easy laugh echoed through the storm; Jax's wild, reckless energy surged with the wind, and Aiden's steady, calm voice wove itself into the cacophony like a ghost of the man who had once held us together.

Now, all those sounds twisted and warped by the ship into something malevolent gnawed at my sanity.

It's time, Sienna, the ship seemed to hiss, its voice rising with the howling wind that whipped across the deck.

You belong to me now—there's no escape.

The air bit into my skin, sharp and cold, as I stumbled onto the deck—the highest point of the ship.

The open sky stretched above me, heavy and oppressive, the clouds swirling like a dark, suffocating shroud.

I stood there on the edge of everything, gazing out over the vast ocean that churned and roared below.

The waves crashed against the hull with fury, wild and chaotic like the storm brewing inside me.

I leaned against the railing, my hands gripping the cold metal so tightly my knuckles turned white. The sea was endless—an infinite, untamed abyss. As I stared out at it, I felt it calling to me, just as the ship had.

It was a different kind of pull, though. The ocean didn't want me the way the ship did; it was simply there, offering a way out—an end to this nightmare I couldn't escape any other way. This was it. The end.

There were no more corridors to wander, no more hallways leading to nowhere. I had reached the edge, both literally and figuratively. I could feel the ship closing in on me, its dark presence tightening around me like a noose, squeezing the breath from my lungs. It had already taken everything from me —Landon, Aiden, Jax.

Their deaths hung heavy in the air around me, pressing down on my chest like a weight I could no longer carry.

Their faces flashed before me, distorted by grief and the ship's twisted energy. They weren't really here, but I could see them—ghostly apparitions shimmering just beyond the edge of my vision. They haunted me, calling to me from the shadows.

Landon stood there, his eyes as soft as they had always been, filled with warmth and love.

He smiled that easy smile—the one that had always made me feel safe, as if nothing could touch us.

"Join me, Sienna," his voice whispered, low and soothing, as though he were standing right behind me, close enough to touch.

"We can be together again. We'll have that wedding, the life we always dreamed of."

A sharp pain shot through my chest, my throat tightening as I swallowed back the tears threatening to spill over.

I could almost feel his hand in mine, his fingers brushing softly against my skin.

He felt so real in that moment, but I knew the truth.

I knew what was happening.

The ship was using him—using all of them—to pull me further into its grip.

But I wasn't going to let it win.

Not yet.

I turned away from the ghostly images, forcing myself to look back at the ocean—the only thing left that wasn't part of the ship's twisted game.

The sea was unpredictable, dangerous, but it was real.

And it was mine to choose.

I took a deep breath; the cold air burned my lungs as I stepped closer to the edge, my feet balanced on the railing, the wind whipping through my hair.

Below me, the waves raged—wild and unforgiving—but they felt like freedom compared to the suffocating presence of the ship.

"I'm sorry," I whispered, my voice carried away by the wind.

"I love you. I'll always love you. But I won't let it take me too."

Then Jax appeared, his smirk as cocky as ever, but something was different this time.

His eyes, always full of mischief and fire, now held a sadness I had never seen before.

They looked tired, haunted.

The bravado in his voice faltered as he spoke, the mask slipping just enough for me to glimpse the fear underneath.

"You know it's easier this way, babe. Jump in. Let the ocean take you. It's better than the ship. You don't want to end up like me."

His voice cracked, the tough exterior collapsing for just a moment.

I wanted to reach out to him, to touch his face, to tell him I was sorry.

Sorry for not saving him.

Sorry for not giving him the life he dreamed of.

But before I could, Aiden appeared beside him, standing tall and steady—just like he always had.

My rock, my calm in the storm.

His gaze met mine, and in his eyes, I saw the deep weariness of someone who had carried too much for too long.

"It's okay, Sienna," Aiden said, his voice soft and reassuring, but beneath the calm, I could feel the weight of what he wasn't saying.

"You're tired. It's time to let go. We'll be waiting for you."

There was love in his words, but also an invitation—a gentle push toward the end.

Toward surrender.

Tears streamed down my face, blurring the faces of the men I had loved and lost.

Their voices, sweet and familiar, pulled at me from all sides.

They wanted me to join them, to step into the darkness with them, to give in to the same death that had claimed them.

I stood there, frozen, my heart pounding in my chest, the

cold wind biting at my skin as I looked down at the black, churning water below.

The ocean seemed endless, the waves crashing violently against the side of the ship.

It promised release—a way out of this nightmare.

I could just… let go.

It would be easy.

The temptation of that thought tugged at me, filling me with the false promise of peace.

No more fear.

No more pain.

No more unbearable loneliness.

But deep inside, something stirred.

A voice that wasn't the ship's, that wasn't the ghosts', but mine.

It was faint at first, a flicker of resistance, but it grew stronger with each beat of my heart.

I couldn't let the ship win.

Not like this.

My grip on the railing tightened, the metal cold against my skin, grounding me.

I straightened my back, determination settling into my bones as I forced myself to look away from the apparitions of my lovers.

Their images—beautiful and broken—faded into the wind as I turned my gaze toward the ocean.

The water was wild and dangerous, but it was free.

It wasn't part of this twisted game the ship had been playing with me and all of us.

It was something real, something I could still choose.

The ship creaked beneath me, its protests growing louder and angrier, as if sensing my defiance.

You can't leave me, Sienna, the voice hissed, sharper now and filled with malice.

You're mine.

You've always been mine.

But I wasn't listening anymore.

I was done letting it control me.

"No," I whispered, my voice trembling but resolute.

"I'm not yours. Not anymore."

The ocean roared beneath me, its wild, untamed energy calling to me with a force I couldn't ignore.

I climbed onto the railing, my feet balancing on the thin edge, the wind whipping through my hair and stinging my face.

Below, the water churned, violent and powerful, yet it was honest.

It didn't lie like the ship—it didn't twist and corrupt.

It was the only thing left that I could trust.

The ship seemed to scream then, the metal groaning in protest, the wind howling as if it were trying to drag me back, to keep me tethered to its dark, suffocating heart.

But I wouldn't let it.

I was done being afraid.

I took one last deep breath, the cold air filling my lungs, and I closed my eyes.

For the first time in what felt like forever, I felt calm.

"I'm not afraid anymore," I whispered, my words carried away by the wind.

And then, with the last ounce of strength I had left, I let go. I jumped.

The wind rushed past me, and for a brief, beautiful moment, I felt weightless and free.

The ship's whispers faded, and all I could hear was the roar of the ocean as it rushed up to meet me.

This was my choice. My escape.

And as the water embraced me, cold and fierce, I knew the ship had lost.

The cold hit me like a wall, sharp and unforgiving, as the ocean swallowed me in one swift motion.

It wasn't just cold—it was biting, a deep, bone-chilling cold that wrapped around me, squeezing every breath from my lungs.

The salt water stung my skin, burning my throat as I instinctively kicked against the pull of the waves, desperate to reach the surface.

My arms flailed, my legs thrashed, every muscle in my body fighting against the crushing weight of the sea.

For a moment, the water claimed me, dragging me deeper into its cold, dark depths.

The pressure built around my chest, tightening with each passing second.

Panic clawed at the edges of my mind, threatening to pull me under for good.

But then, with a surge of energy I didn't know I still had, I pushed back, kicking harder, my hands slicing through the water as I forced myself upward.

The instant I broke the surface, I gasped, my lungs screaming for air as the sharp wind hit my face.

The salt burned my throat, but I didn't care—I was alive.

I sucked in desperate gulps of air, my chest heaving as the waves tossed me back and forth, but I was no longer sinking.

I was no longer part of it.

I blinked the water from my eyes, turning just in time to see the ship looming above me, its dark, monstrous silhouette disappearing into the night like a forgotten relic of another world.

It was massive, a black shadow against the stormy sky, but now it felt distant—final.

The ship's dark presence, once so suffocating, no longer wrapped itself around me.

I wasn't trapped in its twisted belly anymore.

The water surged around me, wild and relentless, waves crashing against my body, pulling me in every direction.

But I was free.

The ocean, chaotic and dangerous, was honest in a way the ship never had been.

It didn't manipulate me or play with my mind.

It was raw and powerful, revealing its true nature.

I floated there for a moment, my heart still racing, limbs trembling from the cold, but a strange calm began to settle over me.

The ship receded behind me, fading into the darkness, along with the whispers, the shadows, and the voices that had haunted me for so long.

The fight was over.

I had won.

I let out a shaky breath, cold air filling my lungs as I gazed up at the sky, heavy clouds hanging low and oppressive. Yet somehow, even that didn't feel as suffocating as before.

The stars were hidden, the horizon blurred, but for the first time in what felt like forever, I was truly alone—and that was okay.

The waves pulled at me, relentless and unforgiving, but they were no longer a threat.

They had become part of the world I had chosen.

A world beyond the ship, beyond the nightmare.

The ocean was my escape; fierce yet liberating, it had given me the freedom the ship had fought so hard to steal.

I tilted my head back, letting the water cradle me, allowing myself to drift as I read the name etched on the side of the boat: Phantom Navis.

CHAPTER EIGHTEEN

SIENNA

The waves slammed against me, their icy grip clinging to my skin and pulling me under like invisible hands intent on dragging me into the abyss.

Each stroke felt like a battle, my muscles aflame, the ache in my limbs sharpening with every movement.

My breath hitched, my chest tightening as I fought to keep my head above the turbulent water.

The ocean wasn't letting me go without a struggle.

But I couldn't stop. I couldn't surrender—not after everything I had endured.

The frigid water gnawed at my bones, numbing my fingers and toes, but I pushed through, my arms slicing through the waves in rhythmic defiance.

The sea roared with violence, towering swells rising around me like monstrous walls, yet out here, in its raw fury, everything made sense.

There were no games, no illusions; it wasn't toying with me as the ship had.

The ocean was merciless, yes—but brutally honest. It demanded survival, nothing more.

I couldn't tell how long I had been swimming; time had dissolved into the vastness of water and sky. All that mattered was escaping, putting as much distance as possible between myself and the nightmare that had consumed me. The cold seeped deeper into my bones, turning my movements sluggish, each breath a shallow, ragged gasp. The salty air burned my throat as waves crashed against my face, stinging my eyes. Above me, the sky loomed dark—a canvas of heavy clouds that mirrored the weight pressing down on my spirit. Below, the ocean stretched endlessly—black, cold, and unforgiving.

But I was free.

That thought flickered in the back of my mind, a small, fragile flame. I had escaped. I had survived. Somehow, against all odds, I had made it off the ship. The cold, the exhaustion, the emptiness surrounding me—it was real. It was tangible.

My body screamed for rest, the exhaustion nearly unbearable, so I finally stopped. My legs barely kept me afloat as I leaned back into the waves, allowing them to cradle me for just a moment. The water rocked me gently, and I gasped for air, each inhale sharp and painful in the biting wind. I floated there, trembling with cold and fatigue, staring up at the sky as the clouds shifted overhead, heavy and relentless.

I had swum so far—farther than I ever thought possible. Slowly and cautiously, I turned my head, bracing myself for the sight of the ship on the horizon, its massive form still looming, still threatening to pull me back.

But the ship was gone.

My breath caught, and my chest tightened as panic surged through me. I blinked, trying to focus, my eyes scanning the horizon for any sign of the cruise liner. But there was nothing. No looming silhouette, no towering structure against the skyline—just the endless, churning water beneath a dark sky.

It was as if the ship had vanished, as if it had never existed at all.

A cold fear gripped me, colder than the ocean itself. My heart pounded in my chest, and my mind raced as I spun in the water, searching for any sign of the nightmare that had held me captive. But the horizon was empty—just me, the waves, and the vast, open sea. There was no wreckage, no lifeboats, no trace of the hell I had fought so hard to escape. It was as if the ship had been nothing more than a figment of my imagination, a haunting dream that faded with the dawn.

My limbs grew heavier, and exhaustion began to settle into my bones. The realization hit me slowly, like the tide creeping in: I was alone. Completely and utterly alone in the middle of an endless ocean, with no way to know where I was or how to survive.

My pulse thundered in my ears, and panic crept into the edges of my mind, weaving itself through my thoughts like a parasite. Was it real? The question hammered at me, relentless, as I floated there, trying to make sense of the impossible. My mind raced, struggling to reconcile what my eyes were telling me—the ship was gone, the sea empty—with what I knew in my bones. Had it all been a hallucination? Some feverish nightmare brought on by exhaustion and grief?

But deep down, I knew better. I could still feel it—the cold, heavy grip of the ship's malevolence lingering inside me like an echo. It had seeped into my bones, wrapping itself around my soul like a noose, tightening with every heartbeat. And their voices—Landon's soft laughter, Jax's wild energy,

Aiden's calm reassurances—still whispered to me, faint and distant, as if they were just beyond the horizon, waiting for me to follow them into the dark.

It was real, I told myself, though my hands trembled as I floated in the icy water. It had to be real.

But the evidence was gone—vanished like a wisp of smoke, leaving no trace behind. The ship, the twisted corridors, the suffocating dread—all of it wiped clean as if it had never existed. And yet the weight of it pressed against my chest, undeniable and inescapable.

My heart sank as I turned in slow, desperate circles, scanning the horizon. The vast, empty ocean stretched out before me, an endless expanse of churning water and ominous skies. There was no sign of land—no boat, no hope of rescue. Just me, floating aimlessly in the middle of the sea, lost and alone.

Isolation clung to me like a heavy cloak, pressing down on my chest and making it hard to breathe. The realization hit me hard, sharp and unforgiving: I had escaped the ship, but now I was trapped in something far worse.

The open ocean.

I kicked my legs, treading water, my mind racing in a thousand directions at once. There was no one coming for me—no rescue, no chance of salvation. The ocean was vast and uncaring, stretching on forever, swallowing everything in its path. I was nothing more than a tiny speck, floating helplessly in its depths.

Hopelessness gnawed at me, sharp and relentless, sinking its claws into my already fractured mind. Is this how it ends? After everything I had fought through, after surviving the ship and losing everything—was this my fate? To be swallowed by the sea, forgotten, with nothing but my memories to keep me company as the waves closed in?

My chest tightened, a sob catching in my throat as I thought of them—Landon, Jax, Aiden. The ones I had loved. The ones I had lost. The ones the ship had taken from me, one by one. Their faces haunted me even now, their voices a constant whisper in the back of my mind, urging me to join them, to let go and sink beneath the surface.

But I wasn't ready. Not yet.

I closed my eyes, the saltwater stinging as it splashed against my face. I fought back the despair that gnawed at me, pulling me under like the current. I had survived this long. I had fought my way free. I couldn't let the ocean take me—not now, not when I had made it this far.

With a deep, shuddering breath, I turned away from the empty horizon and started swimming again, each stroke slow and deliberate. The water pulled at me, dragging at my limbs, but I forced myself forward. I didn't know where I was going or how much farther I could push myself before exhaustion claimed me.

CHAPTER NINETEEN

SIENNA

The ocean stretched out in every direction, an endless, shimmering expanse that seemed to mock my existence, each wave a reminder of how small I was. The water clung to me, cold and biting, as if it had fingers of its own—tugging, pulling, testing my strength. With each passing moment, the cold sank deeper into my bones and soul, wrapping me in its merciless grip. My limbs, once strong enough to fight, were now heavy; every stroke was a laborious effort, my muscles screaming for rest. But still, I floated, unwilling to give in, even as my body begged to stop.

I blinked against the blinding sun, its harsh light cutting through my eyelids. My lips were cracked and dry, the salt stinging each ragged breath I took. My arms burned from the relentless heat, the skin blistered and red—a cruel contrast to the icy water that cradled me. It was as though the world itself couldn't decide how to torment me—burning and freezing, pushing me to my limits. My hands, red and raw, trembled as I tried to move them, but the strength had long since drained from my body. Still, I wasn't sinking. Not yet.

The sea had quieted now, its fury subdued, as if it were waiting—waiting for me to surrender, to accept that I was too weak to keep going. But I couldn't. I couldn't let the ocean claim me. Not yet. My heart still beat; my mind still fought, clinging to the fragments of hope that remained. There was always a choice, and I wasn't ready to make mine.

The pain of my sunburn gnawed at my skin, the heat from the sun baking into my body as if the very sky were against me. My skin, tight and blistered, felt foreign—like it no longer belonged to me. I glanced down at my hands, blistered and red from hours under the sun and in the unforgiving water. They trembled with the effort of staying afloat, but I forced them to move—forced them to keep me alive.

As I drifted, my mind wandered—carried away by the slow, rhythmic pull of the waves. My thoughts moved in circles, always returning to them—Landon, Aiden, and Jax. The men I had loved, the men I had lost. Their faces, once full of life, were now frozen in my memory, haunting me in the space between breaths. Landon, with his easy smile and the way his laughter had always made me feel safe. Jax, bold and fearless, always pushing me, daring me to be braver. Aiden, my rock, the one who had kept me grounded when the world spun too fast. They were gone now, taken by that cursed ship, stolen from me one by one, until I was the last one standing.

My heart ached at the thought of them, the weight of my grief pressing down on me like the waves. I should have given Jax the baby he'd wanted so badly; I should have let Landon plan that wedding he used to joke about. And Aiden... Aiden had believed in us, had believed in me, and we should have had more time. But time, cruel as it was, had been ripped away from us, leaving me with nothing but empty dreams and endless regret.

A wave nudged me gently, as if the ocean itself were reminding me that I was still here—still alive, still floating in the middle of nowhere. The ship was gone, vanished like a nightmare that disappears with the light of dawn. And now, I was alone.

The isolation pressed in on me, a suffocating weight that made it hard to breathe. I had fought so hard to survive, to escape that twisted, malevolent place. But now, in the middle of the open sea, I didn't know what I had escaped to. Was this really any better? Was this how it would end for me—adrift, alone, forgotten by the world? A tiny speck in the vastness of the ocean, lost and unseen?

My thoughts grew darker, the inevitability of death creeping closer with every beat of my heart. I didn't have much time left. My body was shutting down; the exhaustion and dehydration gnawed at me, dragging me toward the edge. But there was a small, bitter comfort in knowing that I had escaped the ship. I had chosen my own fate. It hadn't claimed me, not like it had claimed the others.

Landon. Aiden. Jax.

They were gone, but their memories lingered like the last whispers of a storm. And even as the weight of my exhaustion pulled me deeper into despair, I knew one thing for certain:

I wasn't ready to give up.

Not yet.

A piece of debris drifted by, bobbing gently in the water like a solitary remnant of some distant, forgotten wreckage. It was just large enough for me to grab onto—something solid in this vast, uncaring sea. My hand trembled as I reached out, fingers brushing against the rough, splintered wood. The texture was coarse beneath my fingertips, a sharp reminder of how raw my body felt. I clung to it, using the last of my strength to pull myself closer, desperate for even the slightest relief. When I finally hoisted myself onto it, my body collapsed, weak and limp against the wet surface.

But the relief was fleeting. My muscles were spent, the weight of exhaustion pressing down on me like an anchor. The wood felt like sandpaper against my skin, each jagged edge digging into my flesh, but I didn't have the energy to move. Above me, the sun blazed, a relentless force scorching my already burned arms and face. It was an unyielding fire in the sky, beating down on me, stripping away what little strength I had left. My lips were cracked and parched, each breath scraping painfully through my dry throat. The thirst was unbearable, an agonizing, constant reminder of how fragile and human I was in the face of nature's vastness.

Time blurred. Hours slipped by—maybe longer. I lay there, rocking gently on the debris, the ocean beneath me rising and falling in a rhythm that should have been soothing but instead felt like a slow descent into oblivion. There was no horizon, no distant ship, no sign of life—just me, adrift, floating in a sea that stretched endlessly in every direction, as if I had become a part of it.

With that isolation came thoughts—dark, heavy, inescapable. The ship's whispers still echoed in my mind. It had toyed with me, twisted my reality until I no longer knew what was real. Had it even been real? Or had I conjured it in my mind, driven to madness by the grief of losing everyone I loved? That thought gnawed at me, casting doubt on everything. The ship had taken everything from me, nearly claimed me too, and yet here I was—adrift and abandoned in the middle of nowhere.

I wept for my men, tears hot and bitter as they streaked down my sunburned cheeks. I cried for the love we had shared, for the future that had been stolen from us. For the family Jax had wanted, for the wedding Landon had teased about, for the endless days Aiden had promised. I cried because I would never have those things. The ship had taken it all from me.

But the tears weren't just for them—they were for me too. For the woman I had been, for the loneliness that wrapped around me now, thick and suffocating like the ocean's cold embrace. I was adrift in every sense of the word—lost in a sea as vast and unforgiving as the grief inside me. The certainty of my fate settled heavily on my chest. I wasn't going to make it out of this.

Yet, even as despair clawed at me, pulling me under, a strange sense of peace emerged in acceptance. I had fought. I had made my choice. I had escaped the ship and all its horrors. Whatever happened next—whether the ocean claimed me or I faded into the horizon—it would be on my terms. I had faced the ship, survived its nightmares, and now I was here, still fighting, still alive, even if only for a little longer.

I had made it this far. I had defied the ship and escaped its twisted grasp. As long as I remained here, floating in the vast, unending sea, there was still hope—however faint.

I was still here.

CHAPTER TWENTY

SIENNA

Each blink felt like a battle, my eyelids heavy with exhaustion, my vision blurred by the relentless glare of the sun. My cracked lips split with every shallow breath, the salty air biting into the open wounds. My skin had turned raw, baked to a painful red by the sun, peeling in places where the burn deepened. Thirst clawed at my throat, a constant, agonizing reminder of my fragility. Every muscle trembled with fatigue, drained of the energy that once kept me afloat. Now, I was slipping—drifting into a numbing stillness that threatened to pull me under for good.

The seawater clung to my skin, sticky and cold, a second layer that blurred the lines between me and the ocean. I couldn't tell where my body ended and the vast, relentless sea began. It felt as though I had become one with it, swallowed whole by its unforgiving embrace. No land was in sight, no hope of rescue—just this unending stretch of water mirroring the void within me.

Even as my body surrendered to exhaustion, my mind clung to something else: memories. They danced at the edges of my consciousness, flickering like dying embers in the wind. Landon. Jax. Aiden. Their presence haunted the corners of my mind, ghosts that refused to fade. Their faces drifted in and out of focus—vivid, haunting, as if they were still with me.

I could hear them, too. Their voices, soft and familiar, carried on the whisper of the wind brushing across the water.

"We're waiting for you, Sienna."

The words sent a chill through me, a sudden surge of emotion tightening my chest. They felt so real—so close. Yet they were impossibly far away. My pulse quickened, a fleeting mix of hope and fear—I couldn't tell which—but I clung to their voices as though they could anchor me to something beyond this cold, vast emptiness.

"Landon," I whispered, my voice rasping, barely audible. "Jax. Aiden. I'm still here."

But I knew they weren't. Not really.

I was alone, surrounded by nothing but the endless sky above and the indifferent sea below.

The ship had taken everything—stolen Landon, Jax, Aiden from me one by one, like a cruel thief in the night. Now, after all that loss, I felt myself slipping too. Drifting in this endless ocean, my escape felt hollow, as if I had traded one kind of death for another. There was no hope, no land, no salvation in sight—only the vast expanse of water stretching endlessly before me, as indifferent as my grief.

My body grew heavier, each breath a labor, my eyelids fluttering under the weight of exhaustion. Sleep—something deeper—called to me, pulling me closer to the brink of consciousness. I gazed up at the sky, its blue expanse blurring, my thoughts drifting in and out, wondering if this was how it would all end. Alone. Forgotten. Just another soul lost to the sea.

But then, something shifted.

The air around me thickened, a subtle change that jolted me from the edge of sleep. The wind picked up ever so slightly, and as I blinked against the blinding sun, I saw it—a shadow on the horizon.

At first, I thought it was another cruel trick of my mind—a hallucination conjured by exhaustion, thirst, and the madness of grief. But the shadow grew, its shape becoming more defined as it moved closer. My pulse fluttered weakly in my chest, a flicker of desperate hope igniting inside me.

I squinted, struggling to clear my vision, my heart pounding with the sudden surge of possibility. It was a ship.

A ship.

My breath hitched, and my heart leaped in a fragile burst of hope. Maybe—just maybe—I wasn't lost after all. I tried to move, to lift my head, but my body refused to obey. My limbs were too weak, too heavy from hours of exposure and the strain of survival. I could only watch, helpless, as the ship drew nearer, the name painted on its side coming into focus.

Phantom Navis.

No.

My heartbeat quickened, each thump a heavy, panicked drumbeat. It couldn't be. My mind must have been playing tricks again. But the letters remained, clear as day, taunting me. The same ship. The one I had escaped. The one that had taken everything—everyone—from me.

The ship had returned, come back to claim what it believed was still its own. I wanted to scream, to thrash against the water, to swim as far away from it as possible. But my body betrayed me, frozen in place—too exhausted, too broken. I was trapped, helpless as the ship loomed closer, casting a long, dark shadow over the water, over me.

And then, through the haze of panic and fear, I saw them.

Landon. Jax. Aiden.

They stood on the deck, their figures stark against the ship's looming silhouette. The sight of them, bathed in a soft glow, seemed impossibly serene, as if none of the horrors had touched them—as if the ship had never torn them away from me.

They waved at me, smiling, their faces calm and full of warmth, as if this were all just a dream—a terrible, twisted dream from which I could finally wake. My heart clenched painfully at the sight of them, the weight of all I had lost crashing down on me with a force that stole my breath. Tears welled in my eyes, blurring the figures of the men I had loved, their outlines shimmering like ghosts against the fading light.

"We're waiting for you, Sienna," they called, their voices soft and familiar, carried on the wind like a lullaby. "Come with us."

I swallowed hard, my throat tight as I stared at them, torn between the love that drew me toward them and the terror that kept me frozen in the water. My breath faltered, shallow and ragged, and for the briefest moment, I wondered—was it real? Could I believe what I was seeing? Or was this just another cruel trick of the ship, playing with my mind and tempting me back into its clutches?

My strength was gone. I couldn't fight it anymore. The darkness tugged at me, pulling me under, and I surrendered to it. My eyelids fluttered closed, the weight of exhaustion too much to bear. I felt weightless, suspended between the world above and the depths below, caught in that fragile moment between life and whatever lay beyond.

I had fought so hard. I had made my choice. But now, as the line between dream and reality blurred, I didn't know anymore. Was I still fighting? Was I slipping away, back into the ship's cold embrace? Or had I finally, mercifully, found peace?

The last thing I saw before the darkness claimed me were their faces—Landon, Jax, Aiden—smiling softly, their hands outstretched, waiting for me.

And then—nothing.

The End

If you would like receive bonus chapters or content please sign up to my newsletter here: https://dl.bookfunnel.com/ j0tr34e3km

ALSO BY CASSANDRA DOON

The 4 Seats Series:

Matteo

Felix

Gabe (Coming Soon)

Catcher

Ruhn & Frost (Coming Soon)

Standalone:

The Boys Of Hastings House

The Kings of Willows Peak

Damaged Goods

Tuesday May

The Devils Cut

The Detectives Mate

Bittersweet Snapdragon

Phantom Navis

Obsessed Shadows (Coming Soon)

The Dead Zone (Coming Soon)

Second Chances at The Riverbend Café (Coming Soon)

Still Waters (Coming Soon)

Aces (Coming Soon)

Lavender (Coming Soon)

Dark Dahlia Rite (Coming Soon)

Shadow Prince (Coming Soon)

Ravenwood Manor (Coming Soon)

Summer (Coming Soon)

Oakland Harbour Series:

Missing

Found

Home

Second Chances Series:

The Waterfall

Wicked Bonds (Coming Soon)

The Restaurant (Coming Soon)

Haunted Tales and Withered Old Flowers Series:

A Field of Tulips and Bones (Coming Soon)

Muddy White Lillies (Coming Soon)

The Queens of Shadows Series:

Follow Poppy

Protecting Poppy (Coming Soon)

Crowning Poppy (Coming Soon)